AMERICA STREET

OTHER PERSEA ANTHOLOGIES

More anthologies on www.perseabooks.com

AMERICA STREET

A MULTICULTURAL ANTHOLOGY OF STORIES
REVISED EDITION

EDITED BY ANNE MAZER
AND BRICE PARTICELLI

 A Karen & Michael Braziller Book
PERSEA BOOKS / NEW YORK

Requests for permission to reprint or to make copies and for any other information, should be addressed to the publisher:

Persea Books, Inc.
90 Broad Street
New York, NY 10004

Library of Congress Cataloging-in-Publication Data

Names: Mazer, Anne, editor. | Particelli, Brice, editor.
Title: America street : a multicultural anthology of stories / edited by Anne Mazer and Brice Particelli.
Description: Revised edition. | New York : Persea Books, [2019] | "A Karen and Michael Braziller Book." | Summary: Twenty stories by American authors from diverse racial and cultural backgrounds, including Duane Big Eagle, Naomi Shihab Nye, and Joseph Geha.
Identifiers: LCCN 2018045202 (print) | LCCN 2018051308 (ebook) | ISBN 9780892555017 (ebook) | ISBN 9780892554911 (pbk. : alk. paper)
Subjects: LCSH: Children's stories, American. | CYAC: Short stories.
Classification: LCC PZ5 (ebook) | LCC PZ5 .A5145 2019 (print) | DDC [Fic]—dc23
LC record available at https://lccn.loc.gov/2018045202

Design and composition by Rita Lascaro. Typeset in Stone Serif.
Printed and bound by Maple Press, York, Pennsylvania.

Paperback ISBN: 978-0-89255-491-1
E-book ISBN: 978-0-89255-501-7

First Printing

CONTENTS

INTRODUCTION

When *America Street* was published more than twenty-five years ago, it was the first of its kind. Its goal was ambitious—to capture some of the complexity of what it means to grow up in the United States. It would act as a "meeting place of people and ideas," wrote Anne Mazer in the introduction, offering "a collection of some of the best in contemporary fiction."

The world has changed since then, and this expanded and revised edition reflects that with twelve new stories. Yet our goal remains the same—to explore the myriad ways we live through stories written by some of the most engaging authors across our country.

Reading allows us to slip into someone else's life, opening our eyes to worlds we might not otherwise get to see. We travel through these stories, exploring lives that might be radically different from our own, seeing that a broader world exists and expanding our own world as we read. It is also essential that we see ourselves in literature, that we feel represented, and that we see that there are other people like us. By reading a diversity of stories we are able to grow together, to consider our similarities and differences, and to struggle in the gaps and overlaps between stories and ourselves.

The pieces that follow, each written through the perspective of a young protagonist living in the United States, include classics by Sandra Cisneros and Lan Samantha Chang, as well as work by authors who might be new to you: Tope Folarin, Justin Torres, and Norma Elia Cantú.

They vary across time and in setting. Stories by Duane Big Eagle, Mary K. Mazotti, and Toshio Mori are set in the early twentieth century, while stories by Langston Hughes, Edward P. Jones, and Marina Budhos are set in the Civil Rights era of the 1950s and 1960s. Joseph Geha's story allows us to experience what it was like to be of Arab descent in Chicago and New York City on 9/11/2001, when terrorists attacked the World Trade Center.

Some stories focus on a slice of family life. Gary Soto's is centered on a boy's experience with divorce, Lan Samantha Chang's is about the tales a grandmother tells, and Justin Torres's focuses on dancing, while stories by Naomi Shihab Nye, Susan Power, Sandra Cisneros, and Norma Elia Cantú explore family tradition, and Veera Hiranandani and Rivka Galchen offer insight into how those traditions can clash.

Others center on work, like Francisco Jiménez's story on the difficulty of making friends and attending school when parents move regularly for employment, while Toshio Mori and Tope Folarin focus on children helping their families through new enterprise.

You will see young people caught in struggles that are beyond them, as in Marina Budhos's story of students considering how to protest, or in Michele Wallace's and Edward P. Jones's stories of families fighting for access to a good and equitable education.

Youth is a time of struggle for all of us. We're trying to find a place in a world that is not of our own making, when we must consider what role we want to play so that we might help shape the world we want to be a part of.

We hope these stories will inspire, inform, and empower you.

Enjoy.

Brice Particelli

AMERICA STREET

THE JOURNEY

Duane Big Eagle

I had known the train all my life. Its wailing roar rushed through my dreams as through a tunnel and yet I had never even been on one. Now I was to take one on a two-thousand-kilometer journey halfway into a foreign country!

This particular adventure was my fault, if you can call being sick a fault. Mama says finding fault is only a way of clouding a problem and this problem was clouded enough. It began when I was thirteen. I still have tuberculosis scars on my lungs, but this illness was more than tuberculosis. The regular doctors were mystified by the fevers and delirium that accompanied a bad cough and nausea. After six months of treatment without improvement they gave up.

Papa carried me on his back as we left the doctor's office and began our walk to the barrio that was our home. Mama cried as she walked and Papa seemed weighted by more than the weight of my thinned-down frame. About halfway home Papa suddenly straightened up. I was having a dizzy spell and almost slipped off his back but he caught me with one hand and shouted, "Aunt Rosalie! What a fool I am! Aunt Rosalie Stands Tall!" Papa started to laugh and to dance around and around on the dirt path in the middle of a field.

"What do you mean?" cried Mama as she rushed around with her hands out, ready to catch me if I fell. From the look on her face, the real question in her mind was more like, Have you gone mad? "Listen, woman," said Papa, "there are some people who can cure diseases the medical doctors can't. Aunt

Rosalie Stands Tall is a medicine woman of the Yaqui people and one of the best! She'll be able to cure Raoul! The only problem is she's married to an Indian in the United States. But that can't be helped, we'll just have to go there. Come on, we have plans to make and work to do!"

The planning began that day. We had very little money, but with what we had and could borrow from Papa's many friends, there was just enough for a child's ticket to the little town in Oklahoma where Rosalie lived. I couldn't be left alone in a foreign country, so Papa decided simply to walk. "I'll take the main highway north to the old Papago trails that go across the desert. They'll also take me across the border undetected. Then I'll head east and north to Oklahoma. It should be easy to catch occasional rides once I get to the U. S. When I arrive I'll send word for Raoul to start."

Papa left one fine spring morning, taking only a blanket, a few extra pairs of shoes, bow and arrows to catch food, and a flintstone for building fires. Secretly, I believe he was happy to be traveling again. Travel had always been in his blood. As a young man, Papa got a job on a sailing ship and traveled all over the world. This must have been how he learned to speak English and also how he met Mama in the West Indies. Myself, I was still sixty kilometers from the town I was born in and even to imagine the journey I was about to take was more than my fevered brain could handle. But as Mama said, "You can do anything in the world if you take it little by little and one step at a time." This was the miraculous and trusting philosophy our family lived by, and I must admit it has usually worked.

Still, the day of departure found me filled with a dread that settled like lead in my feet. If I hadn't been so lightheaded from the fevers, I'm sure I would have fallen over at any attempt to walk. Dressed in my best clothes which looked shabby the minute we got to the train station, Mama led me into the fourth-class carriage and found me a seat on a bench near the windows. Then she disappeared and came back a minute later with a thin young man with sallow skin and a drooping Zapata mustache. "This is your second cousin, Alejandro. He is a conductor on this train and will be with you till you get to Juarez; you must do whatever he says."

At that time, the conductors on trains in Mexico were required to stay with a train the entire length of its journey, which perhaps accounted for Alejandro's appearance. He did little to inspire my confidence in him. In any case, he disappeared a second later and it was time for Mama to go, too. Hurriedly, she reminded me that there was money in my coat to buy food from the women who came onto the train at every stop and that there was a silver bracelet sewn into the cuff of my pants to bribe the guards at the border. With one last tearful kiss and hug, she was gone and I was alone. The train started with a jerk that knocked me off my bench and I began my journey upside down in a heap on top of my crumpled cardboard suitcase. I didn't even get a chance to wave goodbye.

I soon got used to the jerking starts of the train, and unsmiling Alejandro turned out to be a guardian angel, which was fortunate because my illness began to get worse as the journey went along. Many times I awoke to find Alejandro shuffling some young thief away from my meager possessions or buying me food at the last stop before a long stretch of desert. He would bring me things too, fresh peaches and apples and leftover bread and pastries from the first-class carriages where he worked. Once, in the middle of the desert he brought me a small ice-cold watermelon, the most refreshing thing I'd ever tasted—who knows where he got it?

To this day, I'm not sure exactly which of the things I saw through the window of the train were real and which were not. Some of them I know were not real. In my delirium, a half-day's journey would pass in the blink of an eye. Often I noticed only large changes in the countryside, from plains to mountains to desert. Broad valleys remain clearly in my mind and there were many of these. Small scenes, too, remain—a family sitting down to dinner at a candle-lit table in a hut by a river. And a few more sinister ones—once between two pine trees I caught a glimpse of one man raising a large club to strike another man whose back was turned. I cried out but there was nothing to be done, the train was moving too fast on a down-grade and probably couldn't have been stopped. But then, did I really see them at all? My doubt was caused by the girl in the dark red dress.

I think I began to see her about halfway through the journey to Juarez. She was very beautiful, high cheekbones, long black hair, and very dark skin. She was about my height and age or maybe a little older. Her eyes were very large and her mouth seemed to have a ready smile. The first time I saw her, at a small station near a lake, she smiled and waved as the train pulled away. Her sensuality embarrassed me and I didn't wave back. I regretted it immediately. But she was back again the next day at a station in the foothills of the mountains, this time dressed in the white blouse and skirt that the Huichol women wear.

She became almost a regular occurrence. Sometimes she was happy, sometimes serious, and most of the time she was wearing the dark red dress. Often I would only see her in passing; she'd be working in a field and rise up to watch the train go by. Gradually, my condition grew worse. My coughing fits grew longer and I slept more so I began not to see the girl so much, but the last time I saw her really gave me a shock. The mountains of the Sierra Madre Oriental range are very rugged and are cut in places by deep gorges called barrancas. The train was in one of these gorges on a ledge above the river and was about to go around a bend. For some reason, I looked back the way we had come and there, imbedded in the mountain with her eyes closed, was the face of the girl, thirty feet high! For the first time, I noticed the small crescent-shaped scar in the middle of her lower lip.

The vision, or whatever it was, quickly disappeared as the train rounded the curve. I sank back onto the bench with a pounding heart and closed my eyes. I must have slept or perhaps I fell into a coma because I remember very little of the last part of the trip. I awoke once while Alejandro was carrying me across the border and delivering me to a friend of his on the train to Dallas. How I got from Dallas to Oklahoma I may never know because I remember nothing. But it happened. And finally, I awoke for a minute in my father's arms as he carried me off the train.

Then, there was a sharp pain in the center of my chest. And a pounding. Rhythmic pounding. A woman's voice began to sing in a very high pitch. My eyes opened of themselves. At first I couldn't make it out, arched crossing lines, flickering shadows. I was in the center of an oval-shaped lodge built of bent willow limbs covered with skins and lit by a small fire. A tall woman came into view; she was singing and dancing back and forth. Somehow I knew this was Rosalie Stands Tall, the medicine woman. The pain hit me again and I wanted to get away but hands held me still.

Papa's voice said in my ear, "She is calling her spirit helpers, you must try and sit up." I was sitting up facing the door of the lodge. There was a lizard there and he spoke in an old man's voice, words I couldn't understand. Rosalie sang again and there was a small hawk there. The pain rose up higher in my chest. There was a coyote in the door and his words were tinged with mocking laughter. The pain rose into my throat. There was a small brown bear in the door, his fur blew back and forth in the wind. The pain rose into the back of my mouth. I felt I needed to cough. Rosalie put two porcupine quills together and bound them with leather to make a pair of tweezers. She held my lips closed with them, painfully tight. A pair of wings beat against the top of the lodge. I needed badly to cough. There was something hot in my mouth, it was sharp, it was hurting my mouth, it needed to come out! IT WAS OUT!

I awoke in bed in a small room lit by a coal-oil lamp. There was a young woman with her back to me, preparing food by the side of the bed. She had very long black hair. She put the tray down on the table beside the bed. As she turned to leave the room, I saw a small crescent-shaped scar in the middle of her lower lip. I started to call her back but there was no need. I knew who she was. An immense peacefulness settled over me. It was warm in the bed. Papa sat on the other side of the bed. He seemed very happy when I turned and looked at him. He said softly, "Raoul, you have changed completely. You're not anymore the young boy I left in Mazatlan." I wanted to tell him everything! There was so much to say! But all I could get out was, "Yes, I know, Papa, I've come on a journey out of childhood." And then I went to sleep again.

THE CIRCUIT

Francisco Jiménez

It was that time of year again. Ito, the strawberry sharecropper, did not smile. It was natural. The peak of the strawberry season was over and the last few days the workers, most of them braceros, were not picking as many boxes as they had during the months of June and July.

As the last days of August disappeared, so did the number of braceros. Sunday, only one—the best picker—came to work. I liked him. Sometimes we talked during our half-hour lunch break. That is how I found out he was from Jalisco, the same state in Mexico my family was from. That Sunday was the last time I saw him.

When the sun had tired and sunk behind the mountains, Ito signaled us that it was time to go home. "Ya esora," he yelled in his broken Spanish. Those were the words I waited for twelve hours a day, every day, seven days a week, week after week. And the thought of not hearing them again saddened me.

As we drove home Papá did not say a word. With both hands on the wheel, he stared at the dirt road. My older brother, Roberto, was also silent. He leaned his head back and closed his eyes. Once in a while he cleared from his throat the dust that blew in from outside.

Yes, it was that time of year. When I opened the front door to the shack, I stopped. Everything we owned was neatly packed in cardboard boxes. Suddenly I felt even more the weight of hours, days, weeks, and months of work. I sat down on a box.

The thought of having to move to Fresno and knowing what was in store for me there brought tears to my eyes.

That night I could not sleep. I lay in bed thinking about how much I hated this move.

A little before five o'clock in the morning, Papá woke everyone up. A few minutes later, the yelling and screaming of my little brothers and sisters, for whom the move was a great adventure, broke the silence of dawn. Shortly, the barking of the dogs accompanied them.

While we packed the breakfast dishes, Papá went outside to start the "Carcanchita." That was the name Papá gave his old '38 black Plymouth. He bought it in a used-car lot in Santa Rosa in the winter of 1949. Papá was very proud of his little jalopy. He had a right to be proud of it. He spent a lot of time looking at other cars before buying this one. When he finally chose the "Carcanchita," he checked it thoroughly before driving it out of the car lot. He examined every inch of the car. He listened to the motor, tilting his head from side to side like a parrot, trying to detect any noises that spelled car trouble. After being satisfied with the looks and sounds of the car, Papá then insisted on knowing who the original owner was. He never did find out from the car salesman, but he bought the car anyway. Papá figured the original owner must have been an important man because, behind the rear seat of the car, he found a blue necktie.

Papá parked the car out in front and left the motor running. "Listo," he yelled. Without saying a word, Roberto and I began to carry the boxes out to the car. Roberto carried the two big boxes and I carried the two smaller ones. Papá then threw the mattress on top of the car roof and tied it with ropes to the front and rear bumpers.

Everything was packed except Mamá's pot. It was an old large galvanized pot she had picked up at an army surplus store in Santa María the year I was born. The pot had many dents and nicks, and the more dents and nicks it acquired the more Mamá liked it. "Mi olla," she used to say proudly.

I held the front door open as Mamá carefully carried out her pot by both handles, making sure not to spill the cooked beans. When she got to the car, Papá reached out to help her with it. Roberto opened the rear car door and Papá gently placed it on the floor behind the front seat. All of us then climbed in. Papá sighed, wiped the sweat off his forehead with his sleeve, and said wearily: "Es todo."

As we drove away, I felt a lump in my throat. I turned around and looked at our little shack for the last time.

At sunset we drove into a labor camp near Fresno. Since Papá did not speak English, Mamá asked the camp foreman if he needed any more workers. "We don't need no more," said the foreman, scratching his head. "Check with Sullivan down the road. Can't miss him. He lives in a big white house with a fence around it."

When we got there, Mamá walked up to the house. She went through a white gate, past a row of rose bushes, up the stairs to the front door. She rang the doorbell. The porch light went on and a tall husky man came out. They exchanged a few words. After the man went in, Mamá clasped her hands and hurried back to the car. "We have work! Mr. Sullivan said we can stay there the whole season," she said, gasping and pointing to an old garage near the stables.

The garage was worn out by the years. It had no windows. The walls, eaten by termites, strained to support the roof full of holes. The dirt floor, populated by earthworms, looked like a gray road map.

That night, by the light of a kerosene lamp, we unpacked and cleaned our new home. Roberto swept away the loose dirt, leaving the hard ground. Papá plugged the holes in the walls with old newspapers and tin can tops. Mamá fed my little brothers and sisters. Papá and Roberto then brought in the mattress and placed it in the far corner of the garage. "Mamá, you and the little ones sleep on the mattress. Roberto, Panchito, and I will sleep outside under the trees," Papá said.

Early next morning Mr. Sullivan showed us where his crop was, and after breakfast, Papá, Roberto, and I headed for the vineyard to pick.

Around nine o'clock the temperature had risen to almost one hundred degrees. I was completely soaked in sweat and my mouth felt as if I had been chewing on a handkerchief. I walked over to the end of the row, picked up the jug of water we had brought, and began drinking. "Don't drink too much; you'll get sick," Roberto shouted. No sooner had he said that than I felt sick to my stomach. I dropped to my knees and let the jug roll off my hands. I remained motionless with my eyes glued on the hot sandy ground. All I could hear was the drone of insects. Slowly I began to recover. I poured water over my face and neck and watched the dirty water run down my arms to the ground.

I still felt a little dizzy when we took a break to eat lunch. It was past two o'clock and we sat underneath a large walnut tree that was on the side of the road. While we ate, Papá jotted down the number of boxes we had picked. Roberto drew designs on the ground with a stick. Suddenly I noticed Papá's face turn pale as he looked down the road. "Here comes the school bus," he whispered loudly in alarm. Instinctively, Roberto and I ran and hid in the vineyards. We did not want to get in trouble for not going to school. The neatly dressed boys about my age got off. They carried books under their arms. After they crossed the street, the bus drove away. Roberto and I came out from hiding and joined Papá. "Tienen que tener cuidado," he warned us.

After lunch we went back to work. The sun kept beating down. The buzzing insects, the wet sweat, and the hot dry dust made the afternoon seem to last forever. Finally the mountains around the valley reached out and swallowed the sun. Within an hour it was too dark to continue picking. The vines blanketed the grapes, making it difficult to see the bunches. "Vámonos," said Papá, signaling to us that it was time to quit work. Papá then took out a pencil and began to figure out how much we had earned our first day. He wrote down numbers, crossed some out, wrote down some more. "Quince," he murmured.

When we arrived home, we took a cold shower underneath a water hose. We then sat down to eat dinner around some wooden crates that served as a table. Mamá had cooked a special meal for us. We had rice and tortillas with "carne con chile," my favorite dish.

The next morning I could hardly move. My body ached all over. I felt little control over my arms and legs. This feeling went on every morning for days until my muscles finally got used to the work.

It was Monday, the first week of November. The grape season was over and I could now go to school. I woke up early that morning and lay in bed, looking at the stars and savoring the thought of not going to work and of starting sixth grade for the first time that year. Since I could not sleep, I decided to get up and join Papá and Roberto at breakfast. I sat at the table across from Roberto, but I kept my head down. I did not want to look up and face him. I knew he was sad. He was not going to school today. He was not going tomorrow, or next week, or next month. He would not go until the cotton season was over, and that was sometime in February. I rubbed my hands together and watched the dry, acid-stained skin fall to the floor in little rolls.

When Papá and Roberto left for work, I felt relief. I walked to the top of a small grade next to the shack and watched the "Carcanchita" disappear in the distance in a cloud of dust.

Two hours later, around eight o'clock, I stood by the side of the road waiting for school bus number twenty. When it arrived, I climbed in. Everyone was busy either talking or yelling. I sat in an empty seat in the back.

When the bus stopped in front of the school, I felt very nervous. I looked out the bus window and saw boys and girls carrying books under their arms. I put my hands in my pants pockets and walked to the principal's office. When I entered I heard a woman's voice say: "May I help you?" I was startled. I had not heard English for months. For a few seconds I remained speechless. I looked at the lady who waited for an answer. My first instinct was to answer her in Spanish, but I held back. Finally, after struggling for English words, I managed to tell her that I wanted to enroll in the sixth grade. After answering many questions, I was led to the classroom.

Mr. Lema, the sixth grade teacher, greeted me and assigned me a desk. He then introduced me to the class. I was so nervous and scared at that moment, when everyone's eyes were on me, that I wished I were with Papá and Roberto, picking cotton. After taking roll, Mr. Lema gave the class the assignment for the first hour. "The first thing we have to do this morning is finish reading the story we began yesterday," he said enthusiastically. He walked up to me, handed me an English book, and asked me to read. "We are on page one hundred twenty-five," he said politely. When I heard this, I felt my blood rush to my head; I felt dizzy. "Would you like to read?" he asked hesitantly. I opened the book to page 125. My mouth was dry. My eyes began to water. I could not begin. "You can read later," Mr. Lema said understandingly.

For the rest of the reading period I kept getting angrier and angrier with myself. I should have read, I thought to myself.

During recess I went into the restroom and opened my English book to page 125. I began to read in a low voice, pretending I was in class. There were many words I did not know. I closed the book and headed back to the classroom.

Mr. Lema was sitting at his desk, correcting papers. When I entered he looked up at me and smiled. I felt better. I walked up to him and asked if he could help me with the new words. "Gladly," he said.

The rest of the month I spent my lunch hours working on English with Mr. Lema, my best friend at school.

One Friday, during lunch hour, Mr. Lema asked me to take a walk with him to the music room. "Do you like music?" he asked me as we entered the building.

"Yes, I like corridos," I answered. He then picked up a trumpet, blew on it and handed it to me. The sound gave me goosebumps. I knew that sound. I had heard it in many corridos. "How would you like to learn how to play it?" he asked. He must have read my face because, before I could answer, he added: "I'll teach you how to play it during our lunch hours."

That day I could hardly wait to get home to tell Papá and Mamá the great news. As I got off the bus, my little brothers and sisters ran up to meet me. They were yelling and screaming. I thought they were happy to see me, but when I opened the door to our shack, I saw that everything we owned was neatly packed in cardboard boxes.

THE WHITE UMBRELLA

Gish Jen

When I was twelve, my mother went to work without telling me or my little sister.

"Not that we need the second income." The lilt of her accent drifted from the kitchen up to the top of the stairs, where Mona and I were listening.

"No," said my father, in a barely audible voice. "Not like the Lee family."

The Lees were the only other Chinese family in town. I remembered how sorry my parents had felt for Mrs. Lee when she started waitressing downtown the year before; and so when my mother began coming home late, I didn't say anything, and tried to keep Mona from saying anything either.

"But why shouldn't I?" she argued. "Lots of people's mothers work."

"Those are American people," I said.

"So what do you think we are? I can do the Pledge of Allegiance with my eyes closed."

Nevertheless, she tried to be discreet; and if my mother wasn't home by 5:30, we would start cooking by ourselves, to make sure dinner would be on time. Mona would wash the vegetables and put on the rice; I would chop.

For weeks we wondered what kind of work she was doing. I imagined that she was selling perfume, testing dessert recipes for the local newspaper. Or maybe she was working for the florist. Now that she had learned to drive, she might be delivering boxes of roses to people.

"I don't think so," said Mona as we walked to our piano lesson after school. "She would've hit something by now."

A gust of wind littered the street with leaves.

"Maybe we better hurry up," she went on, looking at the sky. "It's going to pour."

"But we're too early." Her lesson didn't begin until 4:00, mine until 4:30, so we usually tried to walk as slowly as we could. "And anyway, those aren't the kind of clouds that rain. Those are cumulus clouds."

We arrived out of breath and wet.

"Oh, you poor, poor dears," said old Miss Crosman. "Why don't you call me the next time it's like this out? If your mother won't drive you, I can come pick you up."

"No, that's okay," I answered. Mona wrung her hair out on Miss Crosman's rug. "We just couldn't get the roof of our car to close, is all. We took it to the beach last summer and got sand in the mechanism." I pronounced this last word carefully, as if the credibility of my lie depended on its middle syllable. "It's never been the same." I thought for a second. "It's a convertible."

"Well then, make yourselves at home." She exchanged looks with Eugenie Roberts, whose lesson we were interrupting. Eugenie smiled good-naturedly. "The towels are in the closet across from the bathroom."

Huddling at the end of Miss Crosman's nine-foot leatherette couch, Mona and I watched Eugenie play. She was a grade ahead of me and, according to school rumor, had a boyfriend in high school. I believed it. Aside from her ballooning breasts—which threatened to collide with the keyboard as she played—she had auburn hair, blue eyes, and, I noted with a particular pang, a pure white, folding umbrella.

"I can't see," whispered Mona.

"So clean your glasses."

"My glasses *are* clean. You're in the way."

I looked at her. "They look dirty to me."

"That's because *your* glasses are dirty."

Eugenie came bouncing to the end of her piece.

"Oh! Just stupendous!" Miss Crosman hugged her, then looked up as Eugenie's mother walked in. "Stupendous!" she said again. "Oh! Mrs. Roberts! Your daughter has a gift, a real gift. It's an honor to teach her."

Mrs. Roberts, radiant with pride, swept her daughter out of the room as if she were royalty, born to the piano bench. Watching the way Eugenie carried herself, I sat up, and concentrated so hard on sucking in my stomach that I did not realize until the Robertses were gone that Eugenie had left her umbrella. As Mona began to play, I jumped up and ran to the window, meaning to call to them—only to see their brake lights flash then fade at the stop sign at the corner. As if to allow them passage, the rain had let up; a quivering sun lit their way.

The umbrella glowed like a scepter on the blue carpet while Mona, slumping over the keyboard, managed to eke out a fair rendition of a catfight. At the end of the piece, Miss Crosman asked her to stand up.

"Stay right there," she said, then came back a minute later with a towel to cover the bench. "You must be cold," she continued. "Shall I call your mother and have her bring over some dry clothes?"

"No," answered Mona. "She won't come because she . . ."

"She's too busy," I broke in from the back of the room.

"I see." Miss Crosman sighed and shook her head a little. "Your glasses are filthy, honey," she said to Mona. "Shall I clean them for you?"

Sisterly embarrassment seized me. Why hadn't Mona wiped her lenses when I told her to? As she resumed abuse of the piano, I stared at the umbrella. I wanted to open it, twirl it around by its slender silver handle; I wanted to dangle it from my wrist on the way to school the way the other girls did. I wondered what Miss Crosman would say if I offered to bring it to Eugenie at school tomorrow. She would be impressed with my consideration for others; Eugenie would be pleased to have it back; and I would have possession of the umbrella for an entire night. I looked at it again, toying with the idea of asking for one for Christmas. I knew, however, how my mother would react.

"Things," she would say. "What's the matter with a raincoat? All you want is things, just like an American."

Sitting down for my lesson, I was careful to keep the towel under me and sit up straight.

"I'll bet you can't see a thing either," said Miss Crosman, reaching for my glasses. "And you can relax, you poor dear." She touched my chest, in an area where she never would have touched Eugenie Roberts. "This isn't a boot camp."

When Miss Crosman finally allowed me to start playing, I played extra well, as well as I possibly could. See, I told her with my fingers. You don't have to feel sorry for me.

"That was wonderful," said Miss Crosman. "Oh! Just wonderful."

An entire constellation rose in my heart.

"And guess what," I announced proudly. "I have a surprise for you."

Then I played a second piece for her, a much more difficult one that she had not assigned.

"Oh! That was stupendous," she said without hugging me. "Stupendous! You are a genius, young lady. If your mother had started you younger, you'd be playing like Eugenie Roberts by now!"

I looked at the keyboard, wishing that I had still a third, even more difficult piece to play for her. I wanted to tell her that I was the school spelling bee champion, that I wasn't ticklish, that I could do karate.

"My mother is a concert pianist," I said.

She looked at me for a long moment, then finally, without saying anything, hugged me. I didn't say anything about bringing the umbrella to Eugenie at school.

The steps were dirty when Mona and I sat down to wait for my mother.

"Do you want to wait inside?" Miss Crosman looked anxiously at the sky.

"No," I said. "Our mother will be here any minute."

"In a while," said Mona.

"Any minute," I said again, even though my mother had been at least twenty minutes late every week since she started working.

According to the church clock across the street we had been waiting twenty-five minutes when Miss Crosman came out again.

"Shall I give you ladies a ride home?"

"No," I said. "Our mother is coming any minute."

"Shall I at least give her a call and remind her you're here? Maybe she forgot about you."

"I don't think she *forgot*," said Mona.

"Shall I give her a call anyway? Just to be safe?"

"I bet she already left," I said. "How could she forget about us?"

Miss Crosman went in to call.

"There's no answer," she said, coming back out.

"See, she's on her way," I said.

"Are you sure you wouldn't like to come in?"

"No," said Mona.

"Yes," I said. I pointed at my sister. "She meant yes, too. She meant no, she wouldn't like to go in."

Miss Crosman looked at her watch. "It's 5:30 now, ladies. My pot roast will be coming out in fifteen minutes. Maybe you'd like to come in and have some then?"

"My mother's almost here," I said. "She's on her way."

We watched and watched the street. I tried to imagine what my mother was doing; I tried to imagine her writing messages in the sky, even though I knew she was afraid of planes.

I watched as the branches of Miss Crosman's big willow tree started to sway; they had all been trimmed to exactly the same height off the ground, so that they looked beautiful, like hair in the wind.

It started to rain.

"Miss Crosman is coming out again," said Mona.

"Don't let her talk you into going inside," I whispered.

"Why not?"

"Because that would mean Mom isn't really coming any minute."

"But she isn't," said Mona. "She's *working!*"

"Shhh! Miss Crosman is going to hear you."

"She's working! She's working! She's working!"

I put my hand over her mouth, but she licked it, and so I was wiping my hand on my wet dress when the front door opened.

"We're getting even *wetter,*" said Mona right away. "Wetter and wetter."

"Shall we all go in?" Miss Crosman pulled Mona to her feet. "Before you young ladies catch pneumonia? You've been out here an hour already."

"We're *freezing.*" Mona looked up at Miss Crosman. "Do you have any hot chocolate? We're going to catch *pneumonia.*"

"I'm not going in," I said. "My mother's coming any minute."

"Come on," said Mona. "Use your *noggin.*"

"Any minute."

"Come on, Mona." Miss Crosman opened the door. "Shall we get you inside first?"

"See you in the hospital," said Mona as she went in. "See you in the hospital with *pneumonia.*"

I stared out into the empty street. The rain was pricking me all over; I was cold; I wanted to go inside. I wanted to be able to let myself go inside. If Miss Crosman came out again, I decided, I would go in.

She came out with a blanket and the white umbrella.

I could not believe that I was actually holding the umbrella, opening it. It sprang up by itself as if it were alive, as if that were what it wanted to do—as if it belonged in my hands, above my head. I stared up at the network of silver spokes, then spun the umbrella around and around and around. It was so clean and white that it seemed to glow, to illuminate everything around it.

"It's beautiful," I said.

Miss Crosman sat down next to me, on one end of the blanket. I moved the umbrella over so that it covered that, too. I could feel the rain on my left shoulder and shivered. She put her arm around me.

"You poor, poor dear."

I knew that I was in store for another bolt of sympathy, and braced myself by staring up into the umbrella.

"You know, I very much wanted to have children when I was younger," she continued.

"You did?"

She stared at me a minute. Her face looked dry and crusty, like day-old frosting.

"I did. But then I never got married."

I twirled the umbrella around again.

"This is the most beautiful umbrella I have ever seen," I said. "Ever, in my whole life."

"Do you have an umbrella?"

"No. But my mother's going to get me one just like this for Christmas."

"Is she? I tell you what. You don't have to wait until Christmas. You can have this one."

"But this one belongs to Eugenie Roberts," I protested. "I have to give it back to her tomorrow in school."

"Who told you it belongs to Eugenie? It's not Eugenie's. It's mine. And now I'm giving it to you, so it's yours."

"It is?"

She hugged me tighter. "That's right. It's all yours."

"It's mine?" I didn't know what to say. "Mine?" Suddenly I

was jumping up and down in the rain. "It's beautiful! Oh! It's beautiful!" I laughed.

Miss Crosman laughed, too, even though she was getting all wet.

"Thank you, Miss Crosman. Thank you very much. Thanks a zillion. It's beautiful. It's *stupendous!*"

"You're quite welcome," she said.

"Thank you," I said again, but that didn't seem like enough. Suddenly I knew just what she wanted to hear. "I wish you were my mother."

Right away I felt bad.

"You shouldn't say that," she said, but her face was opening into a huge smile as the lights of my mother's car cautiously turned the corner. I quickly collapsed the umbrella and put it up my skirt, holding onto it from the outside, through the material.

"Mona!" I shouted into the house. "Mona! Hurry up! Mom's here! I told you she was coming!"

Then I ran away from Miss Crosman, down to the curb. Mona came tearing up to my side as my mother neared the house. We both backed up a few feet, so that in case she went onto the curb, she wouldn't run us over.

"But why didn't you go inside with Mona!" my mother asked on the way home. She had taken off her own coat to put over me, and had the heat on high.

"She wasn't using her noggin," said Mona, next to me in the back seat.

"I should call next time," said my mother. "I just don't like to say where I am."

That was when she finally told us that she was working as a check-out clerk in the A&P. She was supposed to be on the day shift, but the other employees were unreliable, and her boss had promised her a promotion if she would stay until the evening shift filled in.

For a moment no one said anything. Even Mona seemed to find the revelation disappointing.

"A promotion already!" she said, finally.

I listened to the windshield wipers.

"You're so quiet." My mother looked at me in the rearview mirror. "What's the matter?"

"I wish you would quit," I said after a moment.

She sighed. "The Chinese have a saying: one beam cannot hold the roof up."

"But Eugenie Roberts' father supports their family."

She sighed once more. "Eugenie Roberts' father is Eugenie Roberts' father," she said.

As we entered the downtown area, Mona started leaning hard against me every time the car turned right, trying to push me over. Remembering what I had said to Miss Crosman, I tried to maneuver the umbrella under my leg so she wouldn't feel it.

"What's under your skirt?" Mona wanted to know as we came to a traffic light. My mother, watching us in the rearview mirror again, rolled slowly to a stop.

"What's the matter?" she asked.

"There's something under her skirt," said Mona, pulling at me. "Under her skirt."

Meanwhile, a man crossing the street started to yell at us. "Who do you think you are, lady?" he said. "You're blocking the whole damn crosswalk."

We all froze. Other people walking by stopped to watch.

"Didn't you hear me?" he went on, starting to thump on the hood with his fist. "Don't you speak English?"

My mother began to back up, but the car behind us honked. Luckily, the light turned green right after that. She sighed in relief.

"What were you saying, Mona?" she asked.

We wouldn't have hit the car behind us that hard if he hadn't been moving, too, but as it was our car bucked violently, throwing us all first back and then forward.

"Uh oh," said Mona when we stopped. "*Another* accident."

I was relieved to have attention diverted from the umbrella. Then I noticed my mother's head, tilted back onto the seat. Her eyes were closed.

"Mom!" I screamed. "Mom! Wake up!"

She opened her eyes. "Please don't yell," she said. "Enough people are going to yell already."

"I thought you were dead," I said, starting to cry. "I thought you were dead."

She turned around, looked at me intently, then put her hand to my forehead.

"Sick," she confirmed. "Some kind of sick is giving you crazy ideas."

As the man from the car behind us started tapping on the window, I moved the umbrella away from my leg. Then Mona and my mother were getting out of the car. I got out after them; and while everyone else was inspecting the damage we'd done, I threw the umbrella down a sewer.

WATER NAMES

Lan Samantha Chang

Summertime at dusk we'd gather on the back porch, tired and sticky from another day of fierce encoded quarrels, nursing our mosquito bites and frail dignities, sisters in name only. At first we'd pinch and slap each other, fighting for the best—least ragged—folding chair. Then we'd argue over who would sit next to our grandmother. We were so close together on the tiny porch that we often pulled our own hair by mistake. Forbidden to bite, we planted silent toothmarks on each other's wrists. We ignored the bulk of house behind us, the yard, the fields, the darkening sky. We even forgot about our grandmother. Then suddenly we'd hear her old, dry voice, very close, almost on the backs of our necks.

"*Xiushila!* Shame on you. Fighting like a bunch of chickens."

And Ingrid, the oldest, would freeze with her thumb and forefinger right on the back of Lily's arm. I would slide my hand away from the end of Ingrid's braid. Ashamed, we would shuffle our feet while Waipuo calmly found her chair.

On some nights she sat with us in silence, the tip of her cigarette glowing red like a distant stoplight. But on some nights she told us stories, "just to keep up your Chinese," she said, and the red dot flickered and danced, making ghostly shapes as she moved her hands like a magician in the dark.

"In these prairie crickets I often hear the sound of rippling waters, of the Yangtze River," she said. "Granddaughters, you are descended on both sides from people of the water country, near the mouth of the great Chang Jiang, as it is called, where the river is so grand and broad that even on clear days you can scarcely see the other side.

"The Chang Jiang runs four thousand miles, originating in the Himalaya mountains where it crashes, flecked with gold dust, down steep cliffs so perilous and remote that few humans have ever seen them. In central China, the river squeezes through deep gorges, then widens in its last thousand miles to the sea. Our ancestors have lived near the mouth of this river, the ever-changing delta, near a city called Nanjing, for more than a thousand years."

"A thousand years," murmured Lily, who was only ten. When she was younger she had sometimes burst into nervous crying at the thought of so many years. Her small insistent fingers grabbed my fingers in the dark.

"Through your mother and I, you are descended from a line of great men and women. We have survived countless floods and seasons of ill-fortune because we have the spirit of the river in us. Unlike mountains, we cannot be powdered down or broken apart. Instead, we run together, like raindrops. Our strength and spirit wear down mountains into sand. But even our people must respect the water."

She paused, and a bit of ash glowed briefly as it drifted to the floor.

"When I was young, my own grandmother once told me the story of Wen Zhiqing's daughter. Twelve hundred years ago the civilized parts of China still lay to the north, and the Yangtze valley lay unspoiled. In those days lived an ancestor named Wen Zhiqing, a resourceful man, and proud. He had been fishing for many years with trained cormorants, which you girls of course have never seen. Cormorants are sleek, black birds with long, bending necks which the fishermen fitted with metal rings so the fish they caught could not be swallowed. The birds would perch on the side of the old wooden boat and dive into the river." We had only known blue swimming pools, but we tried to imagine the sudden shock of cold and the plunge, deep into water.

"Now, Wen Zhiqing had a favorite daughter who was very beautiful and loved the river. She would beg to go out on the boat with him. This daughter was a restless one, never contented with their catch, and often she insisted they stay out until it was almost dark. Even then, she was not satisfied. She had been spoiled by her father, kept protected from the river, so she could not see its danger. To this young woman, the river was as familiar as the sky. It was a bright, broad road stretching out to curious lands. She did not fully understand the river's depths.

"One clear spring evening, as she watched the last bird dive off into the blackening waters, she said, 'If only this catch would bring back something more than another fish!'

"She leaned over the side of the boat and looked at the water. The stars and moon reflected back at her. And it is said that the spirits living underneath the water looked up at her as well. And the spirit of a young man who had drowned in the river many years before saw her lovely face."

We had heard about the ghosts of the drowned, who wait forever in the water for a living person to pull down instead. A faint breeze moved through the mosquito screens and we shivered.

"The cormorant was gone for a very long time," Waipuo said, "so long that the fisherman grew puzzled. Then, suddenly, the bird emerged from the waters, almost invisible in the night. Wen Zhiqing grasped his catch, a very large fish, and guided the boat back to shore. And when Wen reached home, he gutted the fish and discovered, in its stomach, a valuable pearl ring."

"From the man?" said Lily.

"Sshh, she'll tell you."

Waipuo ignored us. "His daughter was delighted that her wish had been fulfilled. What most excited her was the idea of an entire world like this, a world where such a beautiful ring would be only a bauble! For part of her had always longed to see faraway things and places. The river had put a spell on her heart. In the evenings she began to sit on the bank, looking at her own reflection in the water. Sometimes she said she saw a handsome young man looking back at her. And her yearning for him filled her heart with sorrow and fear, for she knew that she would soon leave her beloved family.

"'It's just the moon,' said Wen Zhiqing, but his daughter shook her head. 'There's a kingdom under the water,' she said. 'The prince is asking me to marry him. He sent the ring as an offering to you.' 'Nonsense,' said her father, and he forbade her to sit by the water again.

"For a year things went as usual, but the next spring there came a terrible flood that swept away almost everything. In the middle of a torrential rain, the family noticed that the daughter was missing. She had taken advantage of the confusion to hurry to the river and visit her beloved. The family searched for days but they never found her."

Her smoky, rattling voice came to a stop.

"What happened to her?" Lily said.

"It's okay, stupid," I told her. "She was so beautiful that she went to join the kingdom of her beloved. Right?"

"Who knows?" Waipuo said. "They say she was seduced by a water ghost. Or perhaps she lost her mind to desiring."

"What do you mean?" asked Ingrid.

"I'm going inside," Waipuo said, and got out of her chair with a creak. A moment later the light went on in her bedroom window. We knew she stood before the mirror, combing out her long, wavy silver-gray hair, and we imagined that in her youth she too had been beautiful.

We sat together without talking, breathing our dreams in the lingering smoke. We had gotten used to Waipuo's abruptness, her habit of creating a question and leaving without answering it, as if she were disappointed in the question itself. We tried to imagine Wen Zhiqing's daughter. What did she look like? How old was she? Why hadn't anyone remembered her name?

While we weren't watching, the stars had emerged. Their brilliant pinpoints mapped the heavens. They glittered over us, over Waipuo in her room, the house, and the small city we lived in, the great waves of grass that ran for miles around us, the ground beneath as dry and hard as bone.

HERITAGE

Justin Torres

When we got home from school, Paps crowded the kitchen, cooking and listening to music and feeling fine. He whiffed the steam coming off a pot, then clapped his hands together and rubbed them briskly. His eyes were wet and sparkled with giddy life. He turned up the volume on the stereo and it was mambo, it was Tito Puente.

"Watch out," he said and spun, with grace, on one slippered foot, his bathrobe twirling out around him. In his fist was a glistening, greasy metal spatula, which he pumped in the air to the beat of the bongo drums.

We stood there in the entranceway to the kitchen, laughing, eager to join in, but waiting for our cue. Paps staked staccato steps across the linoleum to where we stood and whipped us onto the dance floor, grabbing our wimpy arms and jerking us behind him. We rolled our tiny clenched fists in front of us and snapped our hips to the trumpet blasts. One by one he took us by our hands and slid us between his legs, and we popped up on the other side. Then we wiggled around the kitchen, following behind him in a line, like baby geese.

There were hot things on the stove, pork chops frying in their own fat, and Spanish rice foaming up and rattling the lid. The air was thick with steam and spice and noise, and the one little window above the sink was fogged over.

Paps turned the stereo even louder, so loud that if we screamed, no one would have heard, so loud that Paps felt far away and hard to get to, even though he was right there in front of us. Then Paps grabbed a can of beer from the fridge, and our eyes followed the path of the can to his lips. We took in the empties stacked up on the counter behind him, then we looked at each other. Manny rolled his eyes and kept dancing, and so we got in line and kept dancing too, except now Manny was Papa Goose, it was him we were following.

"Now shake it like you're rich," Paps shouted, his powerful voice booming out over the music. We danced on tiptoes, sticking up our noses and poking the air above us with our pinkies.

"You ain't rich," Paps said. "Now shake it like you're poor."

We got low on our knees, clenched our fists, and stretched our arms out on our sides; we shook our shoulders and threw our heads back, wild and loose and free.

"You ain't poor neither. Now shake it like you're white."

We moved like robots, stiff and angled, not even smiling. Joel was the most convincing; we'd seen him practicing in his room.

"You ain't white," Paps shouted. "Now shake it like a Puerto Rican."

There was a pause as we gathered ourselves. Then we mamboed as best we could, trying to be smooth and serious and to feel the beat in our feet and beyond the beat to feel the rhythm. Paps watched us for a while, leaning against the counter and taking long draws from his beer.

"Mutts," he said. "You ain't white and you ain't Puerto Rican. Watch how a purebred dances, watch how we dance in the ghetto." Every word was shouted over the music, so it was hard to tell if he was mad or just making fun.

He danced, and we tried to see what separated him from us. He pursed his lips and kept one hand on his stomach. His elbow was bent, his back was straight, but somehow there was looseness and freedom and confidence in every move. We tried to watch his feet, but something about the way they twisted and stepped over each other, something about the line of his torso, kept pulling our eyes up to his face, to his broad nose and dark, half-shut eyes and his pursed lips, which snarled and smiled both.

"This is your heritage," he said, as if from this dance we could know about his own childhood, about the flavor and grit of tenement buildings in Spanish Harlem, and projects in Red Hook, and dance halls, and city parks, and about his own Paps, how he beat him, how he taught him to dance, as if we could hear Spanish in his movements, as if Puerto Rico was a man in a bathrobe, grabbing another beer from the fridge and raising it to drink, his head back, still dancing, still stepping and snapping perfectly in time.

THE FIRST DAY

Edward P. Jones

On an otherwise unremarkable September morning, long before I learned to be ashamed of my mother, she takes my hand and we set off down New Jersey Avenue to begin my very first day of school. I am wearing a checkeredlike blue-and-green cotton dress, and scattered about these colors are bits of yellow and white and brown. My mother has uncharacteristically spent nearly an hour on my hair that morning, plaiting and replaiting so that now my scalp tingles. Whenever I turn my head quickly, my nose fills with the faint smell of Dixie Peach hair grease. The smell is somehow a soothing one now and I will reach for it time and time again before the morning ends. All the plaits, each with a blue barrette near the tip and each twisted into an uncommon sturdiness, will last until I go to bed that night, something that has never happened before. My stomach is full of milk and oatmeal sweetened with brown sugar. Like everything else I have on, my pale green slip and underwear are new, the underwear having come three to a plastic package with a little girl on the front who appears to be dancing. Behind my ears, my mother, to stop my whining, has dabbed the stingiest bit of her gardenia perfume, the last present my father gave her before he disappeared into memory. Because I cannot smell it, I have only her word that the perfume is there. I am also wearing yellow socks trimmed with thin lines of black and white around the tops. My shoes are my greatest joy, black patent-leather miracles, and when one is nicked at the toe later that morning in class, my heart will break.

I am carrying a pencil, a pencil sharpener, and a small ten-cent tablet with a black-and-white speckled cover. My mother does not believe that a girl in kindergarten needs such things, so I am taking them only because of my insistent whining and because they are presents from our neighbors, Mary Keith and Blondelle Harris. Miss Mary and Miss Blondelle are watching my two younger sisters until my mother returns. The women are as precious to me as my mother and sisters. Out playing one day, I have overheard an older child, speaking to another child, call Miss Mary and Miss Blondelle a word that is brand new to me. This is my mother: When I say the word in fun to one of my sisters, my mother slaps me across the mouth and the word is lost for years and years.

All the way down New Jersey Avenue, the sidewalks are teeming with children. In my neighborhood, I have many friends, but I see none of them as my mother and I walk. We cross New York Avenue, we cross Pierce Street, and we cross L and K, and still I see no one who knows my name. At I Street, between New Jersey Avenue and Third Street, we enter Seaton Elementary School, a timeworn, sad-faced building across the street from my mother's church, Mt. Carmel Baptist.

Just inside the front door, women out of the advertisements in *Ebony* are greeting other parents and children. The woman who greets us has pearls thick as jumbo marbles that come down almost to her navel, and she acts as if she had known me all my life, touching my shoulder, cupping her hand under my chin. She is enveloped in a perfume that I only know is not gardenia. When, in answer to her question, my mother tells her that we live at 1227 New Jersey Avenue, the woman first seems to be picturing in her head where we live. Then she shakes her head and says that we are at the wrong school, that we should be at Walker-Jones.

My mother shakes her head vigorously. "I want her to go here," my mother says. "If I'da wanted her someplace else, I'da took her there." The woman continues to act as if she has known me all my life, but she tells my mother that we live beyond the area that Seaton serves. My mother is not convinced and for several more minutes she questions the woman about why I cannot attend Seaton. For as many Sundays as I can remember, perhaps even Sundays when I was in her womb, my mother has pointed across I Street to Seaton as we come and go to Mt. Carmel. "You gonna go there and learn about the whole world." But one of the guardians of that place is saying no, and no again. I am learning this about my mother: The higher up on the scale of respectability a person is—and teachers are rather high up in her eyes—the less she is liable to let them push her around. But finally, I see in her eyes the closing gate, and she takes my hand and we leave the building. On the steps, she stops as people move past us on either side.

"Mama, I can't go to school?"

She says nothing at first, then takes my hand again and we are down the steps quickly and nearing New Jersey Avenue before I can blink. This is my mother: She says, "One monkey don't stop no show."

Walker-Jones is a larger, newer school and I immediately like it because of that. But it is not across the street from my mother's church, her rock, one of her connections to God, and I sense her doubts as she absently rubs her thumb over the back of my hand. We find our way to the crowded auditorium where gray metal chairs are set up in the middle of the room. Along the wall to the left are tables and other chairs. Every chair seems occupied by a child or adult. Somewhere in the room a child is crying, a cry that rises above the buzz-talk of so many people. Strewn about the floor are dozens and dozens of pieces of white paper, and people are walking over them without any thought of picking them up. And seeing this lack of concern, I am all of a sudden afraid.

"Is this where they register for school?" my mother asks a woman at one of the tables.

The woman looks up slowly as if she has heard this question once too often. She nods. She is tiny, almost as small as the girl standing beside her. The woman's hair is set in a mass of curlers and all of those curlers are made of paper money, here a dollar bill, there a five-dollar bill. The girl's hair is arrayed in curls, but some of they are beginning to droop and this makes me happy. On the table beside the woman's pocketbook is a large notebook, worthy of someone in high school, and looking at me looking at the notebook, the girl places her hand possessively on it. In her other hand she holds several pencils with thick crowns of additional erasers.

"These the forms you gotta use?" my mother asks the woman, picking up a few pieces of the paper from the table. "Is this what you have to fill out?"

The woman tells her yes, but that she need fill out only one.

"I see," my mother says, looking about the room. Then: "Would you help me with this form? That is, if you don't mind."

The woman asks my mother what she means.

"This form. Would you mind helpin me fill it out?"

The woman still seems not to understand.

"I can't read it. I don't know how to read or write, and I'm askin you to help me." My mother looks at me, then looks away. I know almost all of her looks, but this one is brand new to me. "Would you help me, then?"

The woman says Why sure, and suddenly she appears happier, so much more satisfied with everything. She finishes the form for her daughter and my mother and I step aside to wait for her. We find two chairs nearby and sit. My mother is now diseased, according to the girl's eyes, and until the moment her mother takes her and the form to the front of the auditorium, the girl never stops looking at my mother. I stare back at her. "Don't stare," my mother says to me. "You know better than that."

Another woman out of the *Ebony* ads takes the woman's child away. Now, the woman says upon returning, let's see what we can do for you two.

My mother answers the questions the woman reads off the form. They start with my last name, and then on to the first and middle names. This is school, I think. This is going to school. My mother slowly enunciates each word of my name. This is my mother: As the questions go on, she takes from her pocketbook document after document, as if they will support my right to attend school, as if she has been saving them up for just this moment. Indeed, she takes out more papers than I have ever seen her do in other places: my birth certificate, my baptismal record, a doctor's letter concerning my bout with chicken pox, rent receipts, records of immunization, a letter about our public assistance payment, even her marriage license—every single paper that has anything even remotely to do with my five-year-old life. Few of the papers are needed here, but it does not matter and my mother continues to pull out the documents with the purposefulness of a magician pulling out a long string of scarves. She has learned that money is the beginning and end of everything in this world, and when the woman finishes, my mother offers her fifty cents, and the woman accepts it without hesitation. My mother and I are just about the last parent and child in the room.

My mother presents the form to a woman sitting in front of the stage, and the woman looks at it and writes something on a white card, which she gives to my mother. Before long, the woman who has taken the girl with the drooping curls appears from behind us, speaks to the sitting woman, and introduces herself to my mother and me. She's to be my teacher, she tells my mother. My mother stares.

We go into the hall, where my mother kneels down to me. Her lips are quivering. "I'll be back to pick you up at twelve o'clock. I don't want you to go nowhere. You just wait right here. And listen to every word she say." I touch her lips and press them together. It is an old, old game between us. She puts my hand down at my side, which is not part of the game. She stands and looks a second at the teacher, then she turns and walks away. I see where she has darned one of her socks the night before. Her shoes make loud sounds in the hall. She passes through the doors and I can still hear the loud sounds of her shoes. And even when the teacher turns me toward the classrooms and I hear what must be the singing and talking of all the children in the world, I can still hear my mother's footsteps above it all.

MERICANS

Sandra Cisneros

We're waiting for the awful grandmother who is inside dropping pesos into *la ofrenda* box before the altar to La Divina Providencia. Lighting votive candles and genuflecting. Blessing herself and kissing her thumb. Running a crystal rosary between her fingers. Mumbling, mumbling, mumbling.

There are so many prayers and promises and thanks-be-to-God to be given in the name of the husband and the sons and the only daughter who never attend mass. It doesn't matter. Like La Virgen de Guadalupe, the awful grandmother intercedes on their behalf. For the grandfather who hasn't believed in anything since the first PRI elections. For my father, El Periquín, so skinny he needs his sleep. For Auntie Light-skin, who only a few hours before was breakfasting on brain and goat tacos after dancing all night in the pink zone. For Uncle Fat-face, the blackest of the black sheep—*Always remember your Uncle Fat-face in your prayers.* And Uncle Baby—*You go for me, Mamá—God listens to you.*

The awful grandmother has been gone a long time. She disappeared behind the heavy leather outer curtain and the dusty velvet inner. We must stay near the church entrance. We must not wander over to the balloon and punch-ball vendors. We cannot spend our allowance on fried cookies or Familia Burrón comic books or those clear cone-shaped suckers that make everything look like a rainbow when you look through them. We cannot run off and have our picture taken on the wooden ponies. We must not climb the steps up the hill behind the church and chase each other through the cemetery. We have promised to stay right where the awful grandmother left us until she returns.

There are those walking to church on their knees. Some with fat rags tied around their legs and others with pillows, one to kneel on, and one to flop ahead. There are women with black shawls crossing and uncrossing themselves. There are armies of penitents carrying banners and flowered arches while musicians play tinny trumpets and tinny drums.

La Virgen de Guadalupe is waiting inside behind a plate of thick glass. There's also a gold crucifix bent crooked as a mesquite tree when someone once threw a bomb. La Virgen de Guadalupe on the main altar because she's a big miracle, the crooked crucifix on a side altar because that's a little miracle.

But we're outside in the sun. My big brother Junior hunkered against the wall with his eyes shut. My little brother Keeks running around in circles.

Maybe and most probably my little brother is imagining he's a flying feather dancer, like the ones we saw swinging high up from a pole on the Virgin's birthday. I want to be a flying feather dancer too, but when he circles past me he shouts, "I'm a B-Fifty-two bomber, you're a German," and shoots me with an invisible machine gun. I'd rather play flying feather dancers, but if I tell my brother this, he might not play with me at all.

"Girl. We can't play with a girl." Girl. It's my brothers' favorite insult now instead of "sissy." "You girl," they yell at each other. "You throw that ball like a girl."

I've already made up my mind to be a German when Keeks swoops past again, this time yelling, "I'm Flash Gordon. You're Ming the Merciless and the Mud People." I don't mind being Ming the Merciless, but I don't like being the Mud People. Something wants to come out of the comers of my eyes, but I don't let it. Crying is what girls do.

I leave Keeks running around in circles—"I'm the Lone Ranger, you're Tonto." I leave Junior squatting on his ankles and go look for the awful grandmother.

Why do churches smell like the inside of an ear? Like incense and the dark and candles in blue glass? And why does holy water smell of tears? The awful grandmother makes me kneel and fold my hands. The ceiling high and everyone's prayers bumping up there like balloons.

If I stare at the eyes of the saints long enough, they move and wink at me, which makes me a sort of saint too. When I get tired of winking saints, I count the awful grandmother's mustache hairs while she prays for Uncle Old, sick from the worm, and Auntie Cuca, suffering from a life of troubles that left half her face crooked and the other half sad.

There must be a long, long list of relatives who haven't gone to church. The awful grandmother knits the names of the dead and the living into one long prayer fringed with the grandchildren born in that barbaric country with its barbarian ways.

I put my weight on one knee, then the other, and when they both grow fat as a mattress of pins, I slap them each awake. *Micaela, you may wait outside with Alfredito and Enrique.* The awful grandmother says it all in Spanish, which I understand when I'm paying attention. "What?" I say, though it's neither proper nor polite. "What?" which the awful grandmother hears as *"¿Güat?"* But she only gives me a look and shoves me toward the door.

After all that dust and dark, the light from the plaza makes me squinch my eyes like if I just came out of the movies. My brother Keeks is drawing squiggly lines on the concrete with a wedge of glass and the heel of his shoe. My brother Junior squatting against the entrance, talking to a lady and man.

They're not from here. Ladies don't come to church dressed in pants. And everybody knows men aren't supposed to wear shorts.

"¿Quieres chicle?" the lady asks in a Spanish too big for her mouth.

"Gracias." The lady gives him a whole handful of gum for free, little cellophane cubes of Chiclets, cinnamon and aqua

and the white ones that don't taste like anything but are good for pretend buck teeth.

"*Por favor,*" says the lady. "*¿Un foto?*" pointing to her camera.

"*Sí.*"

She's so busy taking Junior's picture, she doesn't notice me and Keeks.

"Hey, Michele, Keeks. You guys want gum?"

"But you speak English!"

"Yeah," my brother says, "we're Mericans."

We're Mericans, we're Mericans, and inside the awful grand-mother prays.

SIXTH GRADE

Michele Wallace

I can remember the details but I never do when I think of the episode at all. I remember the feeling and it must have been painful because it hurts now to try to remember the details of exactly what happened.

I had a group of friends that I talked with. All my friends were girls in the sixth grade because the boys would hit you and get your dress dirty. I had never had a group of friends before and I wanted to forget a few things. I had wet my pants at least once every year I had been in that school; whenever a teacher wanted to hit me with a paddle they had to chase me around the room and they rarely caught me and if they did I yelled so loud they had to leave me alone. The kids were still laughing about the latter incidents but I hadn't wet my pants yet this year and it was already October. No one brought that up anymore.

My friends and I had a club that was my idea. You had to chew thirteen pieces of bubble gum every day to join. I loved bubble gum. We weren't supposed to chew gum in class. Of course, I got caught and I had to stay after school for an hour and I cried but the teacher didn't care. So I swallowed a piece of a plastic pen and then I told her. She let me go home, said I should see a doctor. I never did. The piece was very small.

I don't know why my friends liked me, but they were always laughing when I was around so I guess I was funny. They thought I was kind, I think. I screamed at our enemies, cried whenever anybody tried to hurt any one of us. I was different and they liked that, sometimes. I could always tell them things they didn't know already.

I was eleven and I was becoming shy. Before, it never bothered me that every move I made was news for the entire staff and student body of that little lily-white Our Savior Lutheran School way up in the then-safe and silent Bronx. When I reached the sixth grade, it all became very important. I was madly jealous of their little red brick homes in neat little rows near the school with little Dicks, Janes, and Spots running around everywhere, of their housewife mothers who met them after school, of their crisp, immaculate box lunches with clean wax-paper packages of Lifesavers, of their Thom McAn shoes, of their clean white blouses with peter pan collars and their fresh cotton dresses in summer and winter alike, and their white ankle socks, of their small, clear, light print on totally unblemished standard-lined notebook paper in their plastic-covered super-large and cute looseleafs, of their perfect homework in Bic blue ink, and of their little brothers and sisters who were convenient and silent versions of themselves.

Whereas I lived in a tall apartment building with a monumental elevator, all of which was an uncomfortably long bus distance away from the school. I had the El train, other apartment buildings, pigeons who frightened you and did their thing on your head, push-open windows, and kids I didn't know for company. My mother was an art teacher at a public school nowhere near my school, and she used the dinette for a studio, and she and all the walls were always covered with paint. I usually forgot to bring my lunch but when I did, it had been bought at a Puerto Rican delicatessen across the street from my building and it was always a liverwurst hero with lots of mayonnaise and very little lettuce—no white bread, no unwrinkled wax-paper wrappers around Lifesavers, or cucumbers or cupcakes, or anything else; or when my mother made my lunch, which was rare, really rare, it was a ham and cheese sandwich with the bread missing, or the ham missing, or the cheese missing, and no dessert. I was allergic to the milk that everybody drank, which came in red and white waxed containers. Even the teacher drank it, but once in the second grade I had shaved the wax from the container and placed it in a neat pile in the center of my desk where the teacher could see it plainly. I looked up at her frequently, waiting for her signal of approval and admiration of such genius. She hit me with a paddle with a smiling face painted on it. She pulled my dress up and put me over her knee in front of the whole class. She caught me because I didn't run—it was my first year in the school. My lunch was always in a brown paper bag. My shoes were sturdy and lasted forever, no laces, just buckles. Most of my clothes were made by my grandmother—wool dresses in the winter, cotton dresses in the summer, and they were all my grandmother's own styles, styles that no one, no one had ever seen in the Fordham Road part of the Bronx. Nothing I ever wore was pure white, at least not for long. I wore colors, lots of pink, orange, and red, and all together, and lots of crinoline slips and short, short, everything short. I wore tights, no socks. I had them in every color of the rainbow. My teacher hated tights. I know because she told me so, me and the rest of the class. I wrote with my left hand and my handwriting was heavy and crossed out a lot. My teacher told us never to cross out, always to erase. My erasers were dirty. My paper either had no lines, or no holes for looseleaf, or not enough holes but never too many (of course you can never have too many). I never got a looseleaf until at least a month after school started, and even then it wasn't big enough, it definitely didn't have any pretty designs, and I usually lost it. My homework was always done in red or brown ink or with an etching pen, and long-term assignments included my drawings and my own interpretation of the project, and they were late anyway. My little sister, Barbara, wasn't little enough; she was only eleven months younger than I was. She cried constantly, ran up and down the halls, said rude things at the wrong time, wore polka-dotted blouses half in and half out of her plaid skirts, her socks down in her shoes. You always had to repeat things for her twice because the first time she was dreaming. She said things that were not true and talked about me all the time. She pointed me out to everybody she knew, and didn't know, ran after me yelling that she loved me, kissed me goodbye in the morning, came to my classroom and asked for me whenever she could get away, and stood around after school telling me that Mommy said that we should always come home together and right away.

So you see, I was different. Other kids were different too, I know, but everybody in the school didn't know about it. Like this one little Irish girl—her mother was a prostitute and an alcoholic, but what kid knew it in the school? She said her father was the Bailey of Barnum and Bailey and that she was in the circus. Nobody ever saw her father and everybody sat too high up in Madison Square Garden to swear she wasn't in the show. She showed us all pictures of herself with sailors who were her friends when she was little. Everybody did know she was a little different. But my sister and I were first-class entertainment.

I tried to change. I asked my mother to buy a house. Whenever anybody brought my sister up in conversation, I changed the topic to how I had gone to Europe that summer and how good the ice cream was there. They listened and they forgot a little.

But that wasn't enough for the staff of the school (especially my teacher); they couldn't hear me. You see, they looked down on me, and when they did, it was to say something to me, not to hear me say something, except perhaps a phrase from the catechism or one of the hymns. They were not at all happy with me. Although I had a good memory for Bible passages, my attendance was poor in school and in church. My mother was not a churchgoer and didn't have the heart to force us to go. If it rained or snowed heavily, or Barbara and I wanted to be with her, we didn't always have to go to school. In the morning, we would stay home and talk with her and read, and she would put on musical plays for us while we pretended we were sick. In the afternoon, we would go shopping downtown or to a museum or the zoo, or to buy art supplies, or to F. A. O. Schwartz to look at toy trains. When we came to school, we were late, but they didn't kick us out because we could read and write and spell and do arithmetic better than most of the kids who came every day. If they put us in the fast part of the class, we got bored and didn't do our homework and failed our tests, but if they put us in the slow part of the class, we intimidated the kids there. Our marks went from A to F to A, from day to day. Our teachers were in a frenzy. They couldn't say we were non-believers because both of us were religious fanatics, and would render a prayer at the appearance of the merest need. When we didn't go to church, Barbara and I held our own private services on Sunday mornings while our mother slept. Mother told us to lie about church but we never did. Our teachers were dismayed. They couldn't say we were evil or malicious or that we frightened other children or beat them up. We were always disobeying orders, but then we were always sorry, and we would cry until we had proved it. We would give all our money and pencils and lunch (if we had any) and paper (clean or dirty) to anybody. We never hit anyone, we got hit; and when we did, we ran to the teacher. Our teachers were helpless. They couldn't say we were backward because we were extremely vocal and prolific on all kinds of subjects like the Uffizi Galleries in Florence, the New York subways, and Forty-second Street. We did fantastically well on all non-credit tests. We never hesitated to defend our rights, at least not until I was in the sixth grade. Our teachers gave up all hope then.

My teacher that sixth year was different from the rest of the teachers there. She was disgusted and repelled by my sister and me, and she showed it sometimes, too. She was young, about twenty-seven. I think she told us her age but maybe she didn't. I was good at age-guessing, even then. To me, she was striking and handsome, the career girl in the movies. Her eyes were blue; they were cold and at the same time piercing. When she was angry, she would pull her nondescript chin as far as possible into her slender, long, by then strawberry neck. Her nostrils would puff with air and stain red, and it was as if her eyes would reach out with a surgical instrument to pick away at whatever it was in you that was annoying her. She had patience; she had concentration. She would not give up the manipulation of her powerful instrument until either the individual had removed himself or herself from her sight or had repressed that element of his or her character to her satisfaction. One had to give up to her magnetic grasp. To me, in the sixth grade, a little black girl who was used to smiles and hugs and kisses, all of this registered not as an image but as a situation, situation red—danger. I was afraid, scared of her, and I hadn't mastered yet the kind of repression that she demanded; but I was learning. Perhaps if she had gone a little slower with me. I needed time: she didn't have it. She didn't like me. She intrigued me. I know no other word.

She was slim and tall and she stood up straight. Her ancestors were Irish and German. Her name was Miss Kenny the first year she taught at Our Savior Lutheran School. The next year, she got married and she had me in her class. Her name was Mrs. Wernerhann. Her husband was German. The kids who hated her called her Mrs. Watermelon. Her husband came to school for a watermelon party we had at the end of the year; nobody said anything. I don't remember her voice but its quality was crisp, clear-cut with a definite period at the end of each sentence. She talked a lot, not about history or religion, but about the college she went to and particularly her sorority. I was fascinated by her description of her initiation. We all admired her endurance and bravery, and were anxious to prove ours as soon as possible.

I can remember only two things she ever said directly to me. One was about a science notebook that we had to do some assignment in every day, and at the end of the week we had to pass it to her so she could check it. I went to her desk to give her mine. She took it and smiled the only way she knew how and said, indicating pleased amazement: "Your notebook is always so neat, Sandra." Then she looked down at it. There was a gravy stain on the cover. I was smart; I turned my back on her instrument; it felt me but I ignored it. I was silent, smileless. Before, I always smiled. Before, I always had something to say. Now I was silent and smileless. I guess she was satisfied for the moment. She turned her attention to another student.

The other time that I remember, she was indulging in a vulgar habit that all the teachers seemed to have in that school. She was reading aloud the names of each student along with the grade that kid had received on his or her last quiz. There was frequent quizzing in her class. She read my grade. It was one hundred and my grades for quite a time had been one hundred, but it was still quite early in the year. Nevertheless, I did want to impress her. She was impressed. I remember her words exactly. This time I was seated near the back of the room, minding my own business, trying to read my book and forget that she was reading the grades. Other kids were doing likewise or otherwise, but whatever they were doing, all were doing it quietly, very quietly. Mrs. Wernerhann did not permit any noise in her classroom. "Why Sandra, I'm amazed. I thought certainly you would be one of my F students." The class laughed as if they hadn't laughed in years and years and were desperate to find something funny, anything; they would laugh at anything, and this was just as funny as anything. Actually I don't remember how they laughed; it wasn't thunder in my ears, but I know they laughed, I know.

Did she look up my record? She didn't look up my record, because if she did, she would have seen that I'm real smart underneath. She didn't know me before. She only paid attention to her class, only. Did she hear about me? What did she hear? Maybe she heard, but mostly she saw, the lady could see real good.

She was looking at me. Her voice was at attention. She smiled. I smiled. She read the next name, the next grade. She had caught me silent, smileless. I talked only to my friends. I even listened to them more. I never talked to her. I blended more, I thought I was blending. I tried.

It was near Halloween and my class was going to have a party. During our recess period we went to the park near the school. She broke the class up into committees for planning the party. One committee, with all my friends on it, was hanging on the fence. It was one of those wire-woven fences with big empty spaces that we could put our small hands through and climb and pull on. It was inviting; everybody hung on the fence. She was discussing something with one of the committees. I hadn't been placed on a committee; I knew that I should be afraid. I approached her from behind. I tapped her lightly. "Mrs. Wernerhann, Mrs. Wernerhann." I said it softly. No response. I came around to the front. "Mrs. Wernerhann, you haven't assigned me to any committee." I said this softly, too. No response. I repeated my words even more softly, slowly, searching for my error in tone, grammar, pronunciation, attitude. She glanced at me for just a moment, the instrument waving at me: it didn't have time. She continued to address her attentive group who followed suit and ignored me. Actually, I don't know what they did, but they sure didn't stop and ask me what it was that I wanted. I searched frantically—my appearance, my hair, my clothes, my smell, me, me, me, me. This time she had not silenced me. I had come to her silent. It was a kind of victory, I guess, but it was empty. I came without an answer. I was asking. Now my thoughts reached to the end, to the end of that recess period, to the end of the school, to the end of her and to darkness and noise, too, and for now, to the fence, and thereafter I would blend into chairs, walls, whatever would answer my silence with silence.

I went home. My mother always asked me every day what had happened to me in school, and then she would tell me what had happened to her in school that day. We always talked like this. I told her what had happened. She talked to me and I listened to her. I talked to her. We logically figured it out; Mrs. Wernerhann was wrong to have hurt me. Who said pain? She held me. She felt I had a fever. She told me to go to bed. I did.

I cried there, softly so my mother couldn't hear me, although she probably did. I had never cried in bed before, except with a book. It didn't feel like a step forward to be crying in bed without a book as an anchor. I slipped into martyred bliss. I am sure I was not sleeping. I must have been thinking about religion. My bed was my place to think about the "whys" for everything. Why do people look the way they do? Why are there people? Why are there children and adults? Why is my skin black? Now I was just thinking, Why? That was new, too. It didn't feel good. Why? I was asking, why? I closed my eyes. That felt good and right. There were arms around me, my own. I opened my eyes; my hands were stretched out in front of me. Those had not been my arms. They couldn't be anyway; those arms were too large and soft and warm, and I was skinny and puny. And that was not the question, all the "whys" I'd been posing. I had not been answered.

My mother went to school the next day. She spoke to Mrs. Wernerhann about children. She did not ask for love; I didn't understand that. Instead she asked for dignity and respect, placing doubt on Mrs. Wernerhann's professional integrity, rather than on her supply of compassion. Just as my mother reached the door, Mrs. Wernerhann exploded: "Why don't you go to the NAACP?" She had to. My mother was not interested in her silent instrument. My mother, she turned around, she did not speak, she laughed in Mrs. Wernerhann's face, curiously and in operatic tones (as was her manner when she was disturbed), and then left to go see the principal. He spoke mostly of God and love. My mother arranged a meeting with the pastor of our church, the principal, Mrs. Wernerhann, and herself. The two men made silent agreements about the topic for discussion: it was to be God and love. Mrs. Wernerhann was silent. Nobody wanted to talk about me. They asked my mother for her patience, her love and faith. It would take time. My mother did not have time.

As far as I know, I left that school that recess period in the park, but I stayed to the end of the year. I never went back to church. I soon moved away from the Bronx.

YOU DECIDE

Gary Soto

From his bedroom, thirteen-year-old Hector Bustos could hear his parents' voices. They echoed like voices coming down a concrete hallway at a baseball stadium, at a hospital, or the back entrance of a hotel, where bundled trash is tossed into a Dumpster. You open the door, hear freeway noises, and toss.

They were discussing *him*. He could make out his name, but they might as well have been saying "toast, or "bobby pin" or "Doritos." There was not much passion, or nerve, or anything like a tug-of-war. He could never remember them fighting. For years, there had just been a lot of sighing over a toilet seat not put down, or a hand closing like a stone at the kitchen sink when one of them discovered a poorly washed fork. And the laundry? Why did he always hang his shirts so sloppily on the line? And their Lexus? Didn't she know not to park next to a Ford Taurus sure to ding their door?

Hector heard a coffee cup setting back into the saucer. That's how his parents were, nice and tidy, with no rings on their maple furniture. The flowers in the vase were artificial, and the "Great Writers" leather-bound books on the shelf had never been opened. There was an ormolu clock on the mantel, but a spring inside had broken.

"Hector," he heard his mom calling. She called a second time, and her voice grew slightly angry: "Hector, we want to talk with you."

He had already concluded that it involved their divorce. All of his friends' parents were divorced or divorcing. It was nothing new.

"Coming!" he shouted. He breathed in deeply, blew out a lungful of air, opened the door of his bedroom, and walked down the hallway into the living room.

They were there, looking neither happy nor unhappy. It was something in between, like when you get in your car and just drive, your eyes lifting to see in the rearview mirror where you've been.

That's what he was thinking. They get in their car and drive a lot—to work, to the store, to a pastry shop to put sweets in their mouths, to places where he imagined they sat and looked straight ahead. They would look into the rearview mirror now and then and see nothing but blackness.

"Yeah," he said. He stood like a penguin, his arms like useless wings at his sides.

His parents' mouths retracted into small puckers. Neither liked the word *yeah,* but they contained their displeasure. They had more important things to say.

"Hector," his mother started, then paused.

Hector noticed her smoothing her lap, as if she were inviting him to come and sit. But the last time he had climbed into her lap—he was five, he remembered, and he was holding a baby tooth that had just fallen out—she had told him to get down, that he was big enough to sit in a chair. He did as he was told. From across the living room, he'd held up the tooth and said, "See?"

"Hector," his father began. His face was moist with something that was not tears. *What is it?* Hector wondered. *Worry?*

"Hector," his mother repeated. "You decide."

Hector had been prepared by Trent Johnson, a friend at school. Trent's parents were divorced and he'd had to decide who he wanted to live with. Trent had decided to live with his father, who had promised him a bow-and-arrow set. He would get a car when he turned seventeen.

"Yeah, I know," remarked Hector, the new taste of bitterness in his mouth.

At the use of the word *yeah,* his mother winced and crumpled the Kleenex in her grip. It looked like a white carnation.

"What do you mean you know?" his father asked. His tie was loosened, but he still seemed choked by work.

"I just know. You want me to decide who I should live with."

"So you know everything," his mother nearly snapped. She crushed the Kleenex again.

"I didn't say that," Hector risked arguing and added snidely, "I'm only getting Bs." He was surprised how that came out. Was he getting braver?

His father sighed, leaned forward, and palms out, said that they both loved him. Hector had to be mature and decide who he would like to live with. Would an hour be long enough?

"Yes," Hector answered this time.

He returned to his bedroom, where he sat on his bed, a little mousy squeak coming from the springs. He pressed a flashlight against his palm: blood bright, blood dark, blood bright, blood dark. It was a signal to someone far away, a beacon to commandos to land and retake the shore. But he stopped the flashlight game and took a drink of his soda, a hardy gulp that burned his throat and misted his eyes.

"I don't want to be with either of them," he muttered. He looked up at the poster of Alex Smith, quarterback for the 49ers, once a great team but now full of players who fell over like bowling pins. Still, he wished Alex Smith were more than a picture on a poster, wished he could say, "Hector, meet me out back."

Hector had the urge to crawl out his bedroom window into the evening's darkness. The urge became real when he unlatched the screen and backed out, feet first, wiggling for the touch of ground. He scraped his elbow when he leaped to the lawn, as soft as a grave. He dabbed spit on his scrape and moved quickly away from the safety light that had come on.

Alex Smith wasn't waiting in the yard with a squirt bottle in his hand asking, "Thirsty? There was no one, just a small plum tree tossing its head back and forth in the autumn breeze. Hector had helped plant the tree the year before and was scolded because his shovel had grazed the ball of roots. His father complained under his breath that the tree was now ruined, and if it didn't have plums in two years, they would know why.

Hector left by the side gate and hurried away, thankful that the neighbor's dog didn't bark, that his parents were in the living room looking straight ahead or maybe at the floor, the shag rug crushed underfoot.

He jogged for a block and then slowed to a walk. The houses, Hector realized, stayed after a family split up. True, the lawns browned for a while, but there was always fertilizer to bring them back. Flowers could be plugged into the ground and new families would applaud the colors. The sound of the water features outside could hide the screaming inside.

And who ventured out for Halloween? Hector had dressed up as Batman for two years and every time he flew up the steps of a house, porch lights turned off. He could see the flicker of televisions and people ghosting about in their bathrobes. But they wouldn't answer the door. One woman had opened her mail slot and passed him a packet of chewing gum, but she was the only one. No one is nice here, Hector brooded after that experience. You can fall off your bike, and your neighbor turns the other way.

Hector thought of his uncle Rudy, a cowboy type, rough from banging tumbleweeds out of his way, wrestling steer, bucking hay, and spitting into the wind. He didn't think twice about dropping a hatchet on a chicken's neck or about bats hanging in the barn, their eyes red as coals. He hissed at rattlesnakes, hammered fences into the earth, and stared down coyotes that raised their lean heads from the arroyo. He'd told Hector that once, when he couldn't find a razor, he broke a beer bottle and used it to shave his stubble.

Hector wondered how far he had to walk to get to Uncle Rudy's place across town and beyond the railroad tracks. Where he lived was kind of like the Wild West—neighbors yelling, dogs and roosters fighting, radios screaming, mud and mosquitoes everywhere, and the moon always orange and hanging over them. Kids with rickets ate oatmeal morning, noon, and night.

"I want to live with you," he muttered under his breath. He spat. That's what his uncle would have done if he'd been told, "You decide." He should have spat right on the rug, and maybe released a bigger one on the plasma TV.

It seemed to Hector that the orange moon, muscling itself into the tainted sky, was a good sign. That would be his big flashlight, his beacon, his shiny path sparkling with glass. His uncle would be sitting on his back steps, his boots off. Who cared if his socks didn't match or were full of holes or if they smelled mightier than the skunks that came to visit?

"I'm going there," Hector moaned. "I'll live with Uncle." He pictured himself opening a can of spaghetti and eating right out of the can. So what if it was cold? So what if he ate that slop with a knife? He would sleep on the floor and read westerns in which the heroes used barbed wire to floss their teeth. Their combs for their dusty pompadour hairstyles? Big old pitchforks.

He was debating how to find Uncle (follow the banged-up moon to the poor part of town?) when out of the shadows appeared a ragged dog the color of dirty water. Leaves were hooked in his fur. His left ear was nearly gone, one eye was half closed, and fur was missing around his neck. The dog was a refugee, but from where? He had certainly known fights in his time.

"Hey, pooch," Hector greeted and snapped his fingers.

But the dog didn't have time for Hector. He began limping down the street, his eyes shifty in his small head, determined to get somewhere.

"You know where you're going, huh?" Hector sang as he trailed the dog, whose nails clicked on the asphalt. He was determined to keep up with the dog; whether he got to his uncle's place became unimportant. He just felt the urge to journey with a dog that frolicked, fought, and tramped through his years.

A year ago, they had a dalmatian, which had always made Hector think of illness. The dog was quiet. His nose was dry as a leaf. When you showed him his bowl of water, he whimpered. When you petted him, fur came off in your palm. They got rid of the dog when his mother bought new living room furniture.

Hector tagged along, and the dog hurried, scared not by Hector but by something from the east—the coming night when the bats would unlatch themselves and circle the hairdos of pretty girls? The dog was rushing away from badness, or toward goodness, following some dog philosophy of survival.

Hector began to think that the dog had fallen out of the back of a truck and that his instincts were telling him, *Go this way. This way is home.* His own instincts told him to lick a finger and hold it up. *Go where the wind blows, where all the debris gathers along a fence,* he told himself. *Cows will bellow beyond the fence and become your friends.*

The dog suddenly stopped to drink from a puddle. He rolled his purplish tongue over his chops. He sniffed the wind, let his stream flow down the trunk of a tree, and chewed at a flea in his fur. Finished with his doggy business, he began to trot, with Hector in tow.

But three blocks later, Hector paused when he heard a voice call, "Yoo-hoo." An elderly woman was in her driveway, a small stool at her side, in the near dark.

"Me?" Hector replied, pointing a finger like a gun at his heart. He ran over to her.

The woman had locked her keys in her car and had been trying to work a coat hanger inside the window to lift the knob of the lock. She would try, fail, sit down on her stool, weep because no one would help, and try again. She had been at it for nearly an hour.

"Silly me," she chimed, lowering herself onto her three-legged stool and smoothing her lap in a motherly way. Her face was overly painted, her teeth red from lipstick. Clouds of perfume rose from the folds in her neck. She dabbed her brow with a handkerchief and whimpered, "Poor me, silly me."

"Nah, ma'am, it happens all the time," argued Hector. "It really does."

Hector was schooled on what to do with a coat hanger. Uncle Rudy had taught him. It was something, Uncle Rudy had argued, that every man—and woman—needed to master. The old bird of an uncle had also taught Hector to hot-wire a car and siphon gas.

"My son lives in Turlock," the woman said absently. She confessed that he didn't have time for her, that he was a fertilizer salesman always on the road.

Hector noticed that her own lawn was brownish. *Couldn't her son come by and sprinkle pellets on her lawn?* he wondered. Then an awful thought struck him. Was he going to be like her son, on the road forever? Would he be a fertilizer salesman throwing pellets on every lawn except his mother's? The image evaporated as he realized this elderly woman smelled like a flower too close to his face, and that his mother—he winced—gave off a scent of ink. She was a part-time realtor, and what mattered to her was when the ink dried—or so he remembered her saying on the phone.

"There," he said, and opened the car door so he could pull the keys from the ignition.

The woman applauded as she rose from the stool—an ovation for his handiwork. She gave him a pale five-dollar bill, which Hector thought must have gone through the wash. It was soft, clean, and faded, perhaps bleached in a load of whites. Any other time, Hector would have declined the money, but he remembered his uncle, who, if he had appeared from behind that ancient car, would have scolded, "Boy, don't be stupid! Take that money!" It was five dollars for the road.

After this untimely chore, Hector turned, full of panic, because the dog was gone. He called, "Dog, dog, where are you?" He sprinted down the street and found the canine poking his nose into a McDonald's bag. His whiskered face rose from the bag; a French fry hung like a cigarette from his mouth.

The two continued their journey.

Hector followed behind, then moved in front when the dog stopped to sniff a lawn, and finally ended up at his side. They were companions, or so Hector wanted to believe. They were leaving the subdivision, saying *adiós*. His parents—Hector could envision them—would be sitting on the couch, looking straight ahead. Now and then they would look at the clock. Was the hour over yet?

Leaves scuttled in the wind. Trees shook, overwatered lawns leaked, and porch lights seemed to turn off as they passed. When he asked, "It's not far, is it?" the dog, still in full trot, raised his ruined eyes to Hector. Life, Hector figured, is going to send you to mysterious places.

"I'm going to find a real family," he told himself. He was going to a better place, somewhere where he could live with nature, run with dogs, and howl at the moon.

PASSING THE BREAD

Veera Hiranandani

![bird icon]

On the last Friday of most months, Rasika's family drove to Long Island from Westchester to have Shabbat dinner with her grandparents. It took a little under two hours. Unlike her little sister, Aditi, who could read for hours in the car, Rasika got car sick if she read, so she usually listened to music or audiobooks on her phone. If she complained about the length of the drive, her father would tell her he never had a smart phone growing up, while her mother nodded in agreement. Did they truly think Rasika didn't realize this? Sometimes they couldn't go on a Friday and they would go on Sunday, but her grandparents preferred Fridays. They were her only living grandparents. Her other grandparents, her Indian grandparents, had died before she was born.

But this Friday night was not like any other. Rasika felt like a different person down to the blood moving through her veins. She didn't want to listen to anything on her phone. She just stared out the window and watched the gray stretch of the Taconic State Parkway punctuated by tall trees and green road signs.

When they arrived at her grandparents' small yellow house and after they were seated around the table, waiting for her grandfather to say the blessing over the fat loaves of challah, Rasika wondered if they all felt different. She could see a heaviness in her father's face and in her mother's shoulders. Her grandmother smiled a little too hard, or maybe that's the way she always smiled. Aditi sat picking at some dry skin around her thumbnail the way she did when she waited for anything. In general, everything seemed the same, but nothing was the same since her cousin, Sunil, died. He wasn't just her cousin, he was her best friend.

The wooden chair creaked underneath her as she crossed and uncrossed her legs. Her grandfather held up the bread and recited a Hebrew blessing. She didn't understand Hebrew and sometimes it made her feel ashamed. She knew her grandfather had asked her mother to send her and Aditi to Hebrew school. Her mother had said no. Occasionally, Rasika would try to move her lips to the prayers. Her mother was raised Jewish and her father, Hindu. Now they took part in religious holidays only with relatives—Passover, Holi, Hanukkah, Diwali—but didn't practice anything outside of that.

She watched her grandfather move the large knife through the challah. He caught her looking at him and winked. His eyes were an astonishing sea blue and always surprised her with their brightness compared to the rest of him, which was pale and worn. She looked down. He cut the bread with a slightly trembling, wrinkled hand. Her mother told her he had a tremor, but it didn't mean anything serious. Rasika found it worrisome, though, like he lived in a different space than they did, one that was precarious and wobbly.

All this was probably why he said the prayers louder than he needed to. It was probably why he had nicknamed Rasika "Rosie" and Aditi "Adi." It was probably why there was always challah on the table when they had dinner there, even when it wasn't a Friday night. Her father had said one of the first things he noticed when he came to America from Bombay twenty-five years ago was the way people ate bread. In this country people don't tear the bread and pass around pieces, he had explained. Here, we are supposed to eat from our own separate slice, cut with a knife. She wasn't sure if this was true. She had seen other relatives tear apart challah, but her grandfather sliced it.

"Rasika," her mother said in a low tone. "Pass the bread."

She looked at the large silver platter of challah in front of her. Two loaves sat on it, one sliced and one not. She passed the platter on to Aditi without taking a piece. At first it was because she forgot, and then it was because she decided she did not want one. Her grandfather, who always watched everyone closely at his dining room table, noticed.

"Take a slice," he said to her, pointing at the bread. Then he moved the thin gray strands of hair off his forehead and back to their place over his bald spot. She thought of Sunil and the way he used to move his glossy black hair out of his eyes. These memories of her cousin, coming to her in the last few weeks, felt as deep and colorful as dreams. She sat up straighter in her chair to shake the image away.

The day after Sunil died, Rasika promised herself one thing. That she would never lie again, not even to herself. She mostly lied to people by not telling them how she really felt. Was that lying? She wasn't sure. She never wanted to hurt anyone's feelings, but ended up swallowing her own until her stomach hurt. Sunil didn't do that. Sunil was the most honest person she had ever known. He was never afraid to say what he thought. Sometimes she didn't like this about him, but she also trusted him to tell her the truth. She often asked him for his opinions about her friends, the teachers they had, even her clothes. They would discuss the annoying adult quirks of their parents and other relatives. Sunil had helped her figure out the world.

She remembered him telling her once, at his older sister's graduation party, that he didn't like her shoes. "They don't match you," he had said. He meant it as a compliment in a way, that she wasn't formal and fussy like her black patent leather shoes, with little white bows on the front and small pointy heels. Rasika had loved those shoes. They were the first high-heeled shoes she had ever owned. But that was the only time she wore them. If she could go back in time, she would have told him he was right, but she would have also told him that she didn't care. She liked them anyway.

She glanced at the challah again. She never liked it, but always ate a little to please her grandparents. It was too eggy and soft, the dough sticking to the roof of her mouth. Her sister, who loved it, took a huge piece and was already sinking her teeth into it.

"No, thank you," Rasika said, quietly.

"Just take a piece, even if you don't eat it," her grandfather said and gestured again at the platter.

"I don't like it," she said, a little louder.

"Rasika, that's rude," Mom said and narrowed her eyes. The air felt thick and still. Rasika could smell the roasting chicken, still in the kitchen. She could smell the red wine on the table. She could smell the dust under the old green couch in her grandparents' living room.

Rasika hadn't known many people who had died. Her great uncle had died last year, her mother's uncle, her grandmother's brother. He lived in Florida and she had only met him twice. The hardest loss had been their dog, a floppy beagle mix named Daisy. That was three years ago. She had recovered. But Sunil being gone was something she couldn't completely believe, yet it had happened.

She wouldn't believe it at all, except for the pain. She never knew something could hurt like this, could shock her from the top of her head to the bottom of her feet, a full-body lightning strike. Two weeks ago, her uncle had called them on a Sunday night, while Rasika sat on their screened porch, reading her school-assigned summer book and eating a lemon popsicle. She heard her mother moaning words into the phone, *What? No. How? No, no, no,* before she yelled for her father. Since then, the pain only grew, as if Rasika had been possessed by a strange, sagging creature made of rocks and wet earth, like the bottom of a riverbed.

Sunil had drowned in the Croton River, on a summer afternoon hanging out with friends. He was fourteen, the same age as Rasika, and the eighth person to drown in that area of the river since 1994. That's what the local paper said. She wasn't with him. If she had been, would she have been able to stop him? Would she have seen the current in the water that dragged him under? But that was the thing. Sunil always did what he wanted. Even if she had told him not to go in, he still would have. He was on the swim team. He was funny. He was popular. He was the kind of person who was supposed to live forever.

His parents had forbidden him to swim there. Rasika's parents had said the same. Everyone knew it was dangerous, but people, mostly teenagers, still went into the water. Sunil had been in once before. He had told her about it. He went with his two swim team friends, Jack and Brandon. Rasika didn't like Jack and Brandon, especially Brandon. They were always making fun of each other in cruel, stupid ways and laughing about it.

Rasika and Sunil were once talking by her locker when Brandon walked by and said, "Hey brownie, stop stalking your girlfriend." Rasika held her breath for a few seconds. She had never heard the word *brownie* used like that, as a racial slur.

"She's my cousin, dickhead," Sunil said and laughed a strange, loud laugh.

She waited for Sunil to get angry, waited for him to say something more to Brandon. But nothing else happened. She was embarrassed that someone would make a joke about them being anything but cousins. Mostly though, she was shocked that Sunil would let Brandon call him a brownie, would act like it was funny. That wasn't the honest Sunil she knew.

She had looked at Sunil's hands gripping the straps of his backpack. They both had Indian names. They both had darker skin than most of their friends. But Sunil was darker than she was. He had two Indian parents. Was it harder for him? Hard enough that Sunil would fake a smile at being called a brownie because he didn't want to lose Brandon? Was he scared? A wave of nausea floated up toward her throat.

"You okay?" Sunil had asked.

"Yeah," she had said, but she wasn't. He had given her locker a little punch and it shut with a tight slam. Then he had winked. She knew he was trying to act cool to cover his humiliation and brush it off. She had seen him acting like that more and more lately and she didn't like it. She hadn't said anything, just rolled her eyes to show her disapproval and walked away. That was the last time they talked.

Her grandfather stared at her. "It's part of Shabbat, Rosie," he said, nodding toward the platter of challah.

She looked at her father, at his slice sitting untouched on his plate.

"You should respect their rules," her father said.

Something bubbled up in her, something new, something hot and fiery. She looked at her mother's angry but pleading face. She looked at her grandfather, his mouth a straight line. Her father took a slow sip of water and then dabbed his mouth with the white napkin. She wondered what he was thinking. He wasn't an emotional person. He didn't cry at Sunil's funeral, but she had never seen his face look so hopeless, so empty. She had watched her aunt and uncle sob at different times. She had let her own tears fall silently and saved sobbing for her pillow at night.

Rasika turned to her father. "If you respected their rules, you wouldn't have married Mom," she said. Her sister whipped around in her chair and let out a sound, sort of like a laugh, sort of like a yell. The adults froze. It was almost as if Rasika had pressed pause on dinner. Her grandmother even held a serving spoon in mid-air. Her grandfather finally opened his mouth, but then closed it again, saying nothing.

Rasika got up, her heart pumping fast and hard, and walked carefully to the only bathroom in her grandparents' house, went inside, and turned the lock. She closed the toilet lid and sat down on it. She looked around at the pink, black, and white wallpaper. It was an outdated design of circles and squares. Her grandmother's three glass perfume bottles sat on a mirrored shelf over the towel bar across from her. They each were half-filled with old perfume and the amount never changed. She saw a cup on the sink with her grandparents' toothbrushes in it. There was also a shaving brush in a little dish, but she didn't really understand what it was for. Her own father used shaving cream from a can. The sink, toilet, and tub were the color of Silly Putty instead of the stark white she was used to in her own house.

Her words had come out before she had time to think, and now her whole family probably hated her. Her grandfather would tell her mother they weren't invited for dinner anymore. Maybe that's what Sunil was finding, that the more he told the truth, the less he was liked. Is that how things worked? Did people like liars better?

There was a knock on the door. She waited silently. She couldn't tell if it was her mother or her father. Then another knock, a try turning the knob, but she didn't answer.

"Rasika, open the door," her father said.

"No," she replied.

"You're going to miss dinner."

"I don't care. I'm not coming out." She couldn't sit there arguing about the challah anymore. After a minute, she heard him walk away.

Rasika listened to the muffled voices from the dining room grow louder for a few minutes, then settle down. As time passed, she wanted someone to knock, call her name, beg her to return to dinner. She sat on the toilet lid for a long time. She listened to the distant sound of clinking glasses and plates. She heard Aditi laugh. How could she laugh? Rasika wondered if she herself would ever laugh again.

What would Sunil do in this situation? Would he come out or just wait and see what happened? It was as if she had gone so far up a mountain and, with each minute that passed, the possibility of coming back down seemed further and further away.

Another knock, much louder this time, woke her up. She had

moved to the floor, her back against the cold tile wall, and had nodded off without realizing. She had no idea what time it was.

"Rasi," her mother said. "Are you okay? Open up. We have to use the bathroom."

She stood, her legs and neck aching. Her stomach grumbled. When she opened the door, her mother looked at her, this time with sympathy.

Her mother put a hand on Rasika's cheek. "We'll talk in the car," she said.

"Why did you leave me in the bathroom?" Rasika asked.

"Leave you? You refused to come out," her mother said. "We thought it might be better if you took the time you needed."

Better for whom? Rasika thought. "Is Grandpa still angry? Is Dad?" she asked, pulling her mom's hand so they didn't head toward the dining room just yet.

"Grandpa's angry at me, not you."

"For marrying Dad?"

"No," she told her in a whisper. "I don't know why this is coming up all of a sudden . . ." A flush bloomed in her mother's cheeks. "He's not angry about that anymore. But he's still angry at me for not raising you Jewish."

"Oh," Rasika said and thought about it. Maybe her mother should have raised her Jewish. Would that have made it easier? But then her father might have been upset. She liked all the holidays she celebrated. She liked the way they smelled different, had different foods, different gifts, different cousins. Why couldn't that be enough?

"I did it for Sunil," she said.

Her mother knitted her eyebrows together and turned her head to the side. "You didn't take the challah for Sunil? I don't understand."

But Rasika couldn't explain. If she tried, it wouldn't make sense anymore. She shook her head and walked out of the bathroom, past her mother.

Her grandmother called her into the kitchen. She had her

apron on, a faded white one with small green and pink flowers. It was the only apron she ever wore. Rasika wondered why it wasn't dirtier after all these years. She wondered how her grandmother managed to keep everything just so through all of it, down to her apron.

"I saved some dinner for you," she said and handed Rasika a plate full of chicken, roasted potatoes, and green salad. There was no challah.

"Thank you, Grandma." She took it and started to eat, hungrily, sitting at the small yellow and chrome kitchen table while her grandmother turned back to the dishes. After she finished eating and helped her grandmother dry the last of the silverware, she slowly walked toward the living room.

Rasika stood to the left of the archway that separated the living room from the hallway. She saw her father and her grandfather sitting around the coffee table, each with a small glass of whisky in front of him. Her father sat forward on the green couch. Her grandfather sat in his large brown easy chair. They both enjoyed drinking whisky together after a meal. How soon after her parents were married did her grandfather invite her father to have some with him? she wondered. She watched them for a minute.

They talked about something in low voices, looking serious. Then her grandfather reached out and put a hand on her father's shoulder. Her father's face had that same look, a droopy frown, tired empty eyes—hopelessness—that she'd seen at Sunil's funeral. She thought they must be talking about Sunil. She let out a breath she didn't know she was holding and felt lighter. For some reason she had believed they weren't supposed to talk about Sunil tonight. There was even a part of her that wondered if her grandparents knew about what happened. But of course they knew.

She stepped into the room carefully. They stopped talking and watched her. Her father moved over a bit on the couch. Her grandfather gestured that she should sit.

"We will plant a tree in Israel for your cousin," her grandfather said.

She wondered if Sunil would want a tree planted for him in Israel, but she didn't say that out loud. This time, though, she wasn't staying quiet out of fear. It was out of love. Her grandfather was giving what he had to give and he, like the others, had not asked her to apologize for her behavior.

Sunil's parents were in Bombay right now, scattering his ashes in the Arabian Sea near where her uncle and father grew up. She didn't have anything to plant or scatter. There were no prayers she wanted to recite. But she knew the real Sunil, not the one who was friends with Brandon and Jack, and if he hadn't wanted any challah, he would have said so. She had needed her grandfather to see her. She had needed him to know she didn't like challah and still love her. She loved Sunil that way. She didn't want to be afraid anymore, for Sunil and for herself.

"Rosie, I'm sorry about Sunil," her grandfather said. "I'm so, so sorry."

He took her hand from across the coffee table and she saw the water fill up each blue eye, like soft rain over the ocean. She thought of the Arabian Sea, an ocean she had seen only once, and tried to remember if it was as blue. She hoped it was.

HAMADI

Naomi Shihab Nye

"It takes two of us to discover truth: one to utter it and one to
understand it."
> —KAHLIL GIBRAN, *SAND AND FOAM*

Susan didn't really feel interested in Saleh Hamadi until she
was a freshman in high school carrying a thousand questions around. Why this way? Why not another way? Who said
so and why can't I say something else? Those brittle women at
school in the counselor's office treated the world as if it were a
yardstick and they had tight hold of both ends.

Sometimes Susan felt polite with them, sorting attendance
cards during her free period, listening to them gab about fin-
gernail polish and television. And other times she felt she
could run out of the building yelling. That's when she day-
dreamed about Saleh Hamadi, who had nothing to do with
any of it. Maybe she thought of him as escape, the way she
used to think about the Sphinx at Giza when she was younger.
She would picture the golden Sphinx sitting quietly in the
desert with sand blowing around its face, never changing its
expression. She would think of its wry, slightly crooked mouth
and how her grandmother looked a little like that as she waited
for her bread to bake in the old village north of Jerusalem.
Susan's family had lived in Jerusalem for three years before she
was ten and drove out to see her grandmother every weekend.
They would find her patting fresh dough between her hands,
or pressing cakes of dough onto the black rocks in the *taboon*,

the rounded old oven outdoors. Sometimes she moved her lips as she worked. Was she praying? Singing a secret song? Susan had never seen her grandmother rushing.

Now that she was fourteen, she took long walks in America with her father down by the drainage ditch at the end of their street. Pecan trees shaded the path. She tried to get him to tell stories about his childhood in Palestine. She didn't want him to forget anything. She helped her American mother complete tedious kitchen tasks without complaining—rolling grape leaves around their lemony rice stuffing, scrubbing carrots for the roaring juicer. Some evenings when the soft Texas twilight pulled them all outside, she thought of her far-away grandmother and said, "Let's go see Saleh Hamadi. Wouldn't he like some of that cheese pie Mom made?" And they would wrap a slice of pie and drive downtown. Somehow he felt like a good substitute for a grandmother, even though he was a man.

Usually Hamadi was wearing a white shirt, shiny black tie, and a jacket that reminded Susan of the earth's surface just above the treeline on a mountain—thin, somehow purified. He would raise his hands high before giving advice.

"It is good to drink a tall glass of water every morning upon arising!" If anyone doubted this, he would shake his head. "Oh Susan, Susan, Susan," he would say.

He did not like to sit down, but he wanted everyone else to sit down. He made Susan sit on the wobbly chair beside the desk and he made her father or mother sit in the saggy center of the bed. He told them people should eat six small meals a day.

They visited him on the sixth floor of the Traveler's Hotel, where he had lived so long nobody could remember him ever traveling. Susan's father used to remind him of the apartments available over the Victory Cleaners, next to the park with the fizzy pink fountain, but Hamadi would shake his head, pinching kisses at his spartan room. "A white handkerchief spread across a tabletop, my two extra shoes lined by the wall, this spells 'home' to me, this says 'mi casa.' What more do I need?"

Hamadi liked to use Spanish words. They made him feel expansive, worldly. He'd learned them when he worked at the fruits and vegetables warehouse on Zarzamora Street, marking off crates of apples and avocados on a long white pad. Occasionally he would speak Arabic, his own first language, with Susan's father and uncles, but he said it made him feel too sad, as if his mother might step into the room at any minute, her arms laden with fresh mint leaves. He had come to the United States on a boat when he was eighteen years old and he had never been married. "l married books," he said. "I married the wide horizon."

"What is he to us?" Susan used to ask her father. "He's not a relative, right? How did we meet him to begin with?"

Susan's father couldn't remember. "I think we just drifted together. Maybe we met at your uncle Hani's house. Maybe that old Maronite priest who used to cry after every service introduced us. The priest once shared an apartment with Kahlil Gibran in New York—so he said. And Saleh always says he stayed with Gibran when he first got off the boat. I'll bet that popular guy Gibran has had a lot of roommates he doesn't even know about."

Susan said, "Dad, he's dead."

"I know, I know," her father said.

Later Susan said, "Mr. Hamadi, did you really meet Kahlil Gibran? He's one of my favorite writers." Hamadi walked slowly to the window of his room and stared out. There wasn't much to look at down on the street—a bedraggled flower shop, a boarded-up tavern with a hand-lettered sign tacked to the front, GONE TO FIND JESUS. Susan's father said the owners had really gone to Alabama.

Hamadi spoke patiently. "Yes, I met brother Gibran. And I meet him in my heart every day. When I was a young man—shocked by all the visions of the new world—the tall buildings—the wild traffic—the young people without shame—the proud mailboxes in their blue uniforms—I met him. And he has stayed with me every day of my life."

"But did you really meet him, like in person, or just in a book?"

He turned dramatically. "Make no such distinctions, my friend. Or your life will be a pod with only dried-up beans inside. Believe anything can happen."

Susan's father looked irritated, but Susan smiled. "I do," she said. "I believe that. I want fat beans. If I imagine something, it's true, too. Just a different kind of true."

Susan's father was twiddling with the knobs on the old-fashioned sink. "Don't they even give you hot water here? You don't mean to tell me you've been living without hot water?"

On Hamadi's rickety desk lay a row of different "Love" stamps issued by the post office.

"You must write a lot of letters," Susan said.

"No, no, I'm just focusing on that word," Hamadi said. "I particularly like the globe in the shape of a heart," he added.

"Why don't you take a trip back to your village in Lebanon?" Susan's father asked. "Maybe you still have relatives living there."

Hamadi looked pained. "'Remembrance is a form of meeting,' my brother Gibran says, and I do believe I meet with my cousins every day."

"But aren't you curious? You've been gone so long! Wouldn't you like to find out what has happened to everybody and everything you knew as a boy?" Susan's father traveled back to Jerusalem once each year to see his family.

"I would not. In fact, I already know. It is there and it is not there. Would you like to share an orange with me?"

His long fingers, tenderly peeling. Once when Susan was younger, he'd given her a lavish ribbon off a holiday fruit basket and expected her to wear it on her head. In the car, Susan's father said, "Riddles. He talks in riddles. I don't know why I have patience with him." Susan stared at the people talking and laughing in the next car. She did not even exist in their world.

Susan carried *The Prophet* around on top of her English text-book and her Texas history. She and her friend Tracy read it out loud to one another at lunch. Tracy was a junior—they'd met at the literary magazine meeting where Susan, the only freshman on the staff, got assigned to do proofreading. They never ate in the cafeteria; they sat outside at picnic tables with sack lunches, whole wheat crackers and fresh peaches. Both of them had given up meat.

Tracy's eyes looked steamy. "You know that place where Gibran says, 'Hate is a dead thing. Who of you would be a tomb?'"

Susan nodded. Tracy continued. "Well, I hate someone. I'm trying not to, but I can't help it. l hate Debbie for liking Eddie and it's driving me nuts."

"Why shouldn't Debbie like Eddie?" Susan said. "*You* do."

Tracy put her head down on her arms. A gang of cheer-leaders walked by giggling. One of them flicked her finger in greeting.

"In fact, we *all* like Eddie," Susan said. "Remember, here in this book—wait and I'll find it—where Gibran says that loving teaches us the secrets of our hearts and that's the way we con-nect to all of Life's heart? You're not talking about liking or loving, you're talking about owning."

Tracy looked glum. "Sometimes you remind me of a minister."

Susan said, "Well, just talk to me someday when *I'm* depressed."

Susan didn't want a boyfriend. Everyone who had boy-friends or girlfriends seemed to have troubles. Susan told peo-ple she had a boyfriend far away, on a farm in Missouri, but the truth was, boys still seemed like cousins to her. Or brothers. Or even girls.

A squirrel sat in the crook of a tree, eyeing their sand-wiches. When the end-of-lunch bell blared, Susan and Tracy jumped—it always seemed too soon. Squirrels were lucky; they didn't have to go to school.

Susan's father said her idea was ridiculous: to invite Saleh Hamadi to go Christmas caroling with the English Club. "His English is archaic, for one thing, and he won't know *any* of the songs.

"'How could you live in America for years and not know 'Joy to the World' or 'Away in a Manger'?"

"Listen, I grew up right down the road from 'Oh Little Town of Bethlehem' and I still don't know a single verse."

"I want him. We need him. It's boring being with the same bunch of people all the time."

So they called Saleh and he said he would come—"thrilled" was the word he used. He wanted to ride the bus to their house, he didn't want anyone to pick him up. Her father muttered, "He'll probably forget to get off." Saleh thought "caroling" meant they were going out with a woman named Carol. He said, "Holiday spirit—I was just reading about it in the newspaper."

Susan said, "Dress warm."

Saleh replied, "Friend, my heart is warmed simply to hear your voice."

All that evening Susan felt light and bouncy. She decorated the coffee can they would use to collect donations to be sent to the children's hospital in Bethlehem. She had started doing this last year in middle school, when a singing group collected one hundred dollars, and the hospital responded on exotic onion-skin stationery that they were "eternally grateful."

Her father shook his head. "You get something into your mind and it really takes over," he said. "Why do you like Hamadi so much all of a sudden? You could show half as much interest in your own uncles."

Susan laughed. Her uncles were dull. Her uncles shopped at the mall and watched TV. "Anyone who watches TV more than twelve minutes a week is uninteresting," she said.

Her father lifted an eyebrow.

"He's my surrogate grandmother," she said. "He says interesting things. He makes me think. Remember when I was little and he called me The Thinker? We have a connection." She added, "Listen, do you want to go too? It's not a big deal. And Mom has a *great* voice. Why don't you both come?"

A minute later her mother was digging in the closet for neck scarves, and her father was digging in the drawer for flashlight batteries.

Saleh Hamadi arrived precisely on time, with flushed red cheeks and a sack of dates stuffed in his pocket. "We may need sustenance on our journey." Susan thought the older people seemed quite giddy as they drove down to the high school to meet the rest of the carolers. Strands of winking lights wrapped around their neighbors' drainpipes and trees. A giant Santa tipped his hat on Dr. Garcia's roof.

Her friends stood gathered in front of the school. Some were smoothing out song sheets that had been crammed in a drawer or cabinet for a whole year. Susan thought holidays were strange; they came, and you were supposed to feel ready for them. What if you could make up your own holidays as you went along? She had read about a woman who used to have parties to celebrate the arrival of fresh asparagus in the local market. Susan's friends might make holidays called Eddie Looked at Me Today and Smiled.

Two people were alleluia-ing in harmony. Saleh Hamadi went around the group formally introducing himself to each person and shaking hands. A few people laughed silently when his back was turned. He had stepped out of a painting, or a newscast, with his outdated long overcoat, his clunky old man's shoes and elegant manners.

Susan spoke more loudly than usual. "I'm honored to introduce you to one of my best friends, Mr. Hamadi."

"Good evening to you," he pronounced musically, bowing a bit from the waist.

What could you say back but "Good evening, sir." His old-fashioned manners were contagious.

They sang at three houses that never opened their doors. They sang "We Wish You a Merry Christmas" each time they moved on. Lisa had a fine, clear soprano. Tracy could find the alto harmony to any line. Cameron and Elliot had more enthusiasm than accuracy. Lily, Rita, and Jeannette laughed every time they said a wrong word and fumbled to find their places again. Susan loved to see how her mother knew every word of every verse without looking at the paper, and how her father kept his hands in his pockets and seemed more interested in examining people's mailboxes or yard displays than in trying to sing. And Saleh Hamadi—what language was he singing in? He didn't even seem to be pronouncing words, but humming deeply from his throat. Was he saying, "Om"? Speaking Arabic? Once he caught her looking and whispered, "That was an Aramaic word that just drifted into my mouth— the true language of the Bible, you know, the language Jesus Christ himself spoke."

By the fourth block their voices felt tuned up and friendly people came outside to listen. Trays of cookies were passed around and dollar bills stuffed into the little can. Thank you, thank you. Out of the dark from down the block, Susan noticed Eddie sprinting toward them with his coat flapping, unbuttoned. She shot a glance at Tracy, who pretended not to notice. "Hey, guys!" shouted Eddie. "The first time in my life I'm late and everyone else is on time! You could at least have left a note about which way you were going." Someone slapped him on the back. Saleh Hamadi, whom he had never seen before, was the only one who managed a reply. "Welcome, welcome to our cheery group!"

Eddie looked mystified. "Who is this guy?"

Susan whispered, "My friend."

Eddie approached Tracy, who read her song sheet intently just then, and stuck his face over her shoulder to whisper, "Hi."

Tracy stared straight ahead into the air and whispered "Hi" vaguely, glumly. Susan shook her head. Couldn't Tracy act more cheerful at least?

They were walking again. They passed a string of blinking reindeer and a wooden snowman holding a painted candle.

Eddie fell into step beside Tracy, murmuring so Susan couldn't hear him anymore. Saleh Hamadi was flinging his arms up high as he strode. Was he power walking? Did he even know what power walking was? Between houses, Susan's mother hummed obscure songs people hardly remembered: "What Child Is This?" and "The Friendly Beasts."

Lisa moved over to Eddie's other side. "I'm *so excited* about you and Debbie!" she said loudly. "Why didn't she come tonight?"

Eddie said, "She has a sore throat."

Tracy shrank up inside her coat.

Lisa chattered on. "James said we should make our reservations *now* for dinner at the Tower after the Sweetheart Dance, can you believe it? In December, making a reservation for February? But otherwise it might get booked up!"

Saleh Hamadi tuned into this conversation with interest; the Tower was downtown, in his neighborhood. He said, "This sounds like significant preliminary planning! Maybe you can be an international advisor someday." Susan's mother bellowed, "Joy to the World!" and voices followed her, stretching for notes. Susan's father was gazing off into the sky. Maybe he thought about all the refugees in camps in Palestine far from doorbells and shutters. Maybe he thought about the horizon beyond Jerusalem when he was a boy, how it seemed to be inviting him, "Come over, come over." Well, he'd come all the way to the other side of the world, and now he was doomed to live in two places at once. To Susan, immigrants seemed bigger than other people, and always slightly melancholy. They also seemed doubly interesting. Maybe someday Susan would meet one her own age.

Two thin streams of tears rolled down Tracy's face. Eddie had drifted to the other side of the group and was clowning with Cameron, doing a tap dance shuffle. "While fields and floods, rocks, hills and plains, repeat the sounding joy, repeat the sounding joy..." Susan and Saleh Hamadi noticed her. Hamadi peered into Tracy's face, inquiring, "Why? Is it pain? Is it gratitude? We are such mysterious creatures, human beings!"

Tracy turned to him, pressing her face against the old wool of his coat, and wailed. The song ended. All eyes were on Tracy and this tall, courteous stranger who would never in a thousand years have felt comfortable stroking her hair. But he let her stand there, crying, as Susan stepped up firmly on the other side of Tracy, putting her arms around her friend. And Hamadi said something Susan would remember years later, whenever she was sad herself, even after college, a creaky anthem sneaking back into her ear, "We go on. On and on. We don't stop where it hurts. We turn a corner. It is the reason why we are living. To turn a corner. Come, let's move."

Above them, in the heavens, stars lived out their lonely lives. People whispered, "What happened? What's wrong?" Half of them were already walking down the street.

DRUM KISS

Susan Power

E ven though I am eleven years old, which Grandma Lizzie
says means I am practically a woman, I'm still looking for
the entrance to another world at the back of her closet. I read
these books by an Englishman named C. S. Lewis, my favorite
one being *The Lion, the Witch, and the Wardrobe,* where four
children find their way to a country called Narnia by walking
into a large wardrobe and wading through the fur coats stored
inside. Grandma Lizzie and I don't have a wardrobe, I don't
think I've ever seen one in real life, we don't have fur coats,
and there's just one clothes closet in our basement apartment,
but I check it out every night before going to bed. This act is
the moment of possible magic I live for, and my heart pounds
every time I open the heavy door and step inside, hands grop-
ing forward in the dark to part our few garments hanging there
before me, fingers tingling with excitement as they stretch and
reach, poke past the clothes, stretch and reach again, only to
graze the pebbly painted wall at the back. I haven't found the
portal yet, but still I believe. I believe in magic and miracles
and ghosts and witches. I believe there has to be a way out of
this place. It's not that I would leave Grandma Lizzie behind
forever. If I found my way into what the books call a "magi-
cal realm," I'd work to discover a potion that would cure my
grandmother, and I'd bring it back to her and spoon it in her
mouth. I would be a princess by this time, so she would listen
to me and drink what I asked her to, without questions. She
would obey me because she would hear the grand authority

in my voice, the confidence, the kindness, the shining intelligence. Then Grandma Lizzie would be transformed into her younger self—the one I have spied in her photograph albums. I picture her the way she looked at a fancy nightclub costume party where she dressed as one of those Spanish dancers who does the flamenco, wearing a long, tight dress with tiny polka dots on the fabric and huge foamy ruffles at the hem. Her hair was pulled back in a bun framed by large tortoiseshell combs, and she'd pasted dramatic curls of hair to her forehead. Her hands were in motion, though she was posing for the camera, fingers clicking castanets so energetically I could always *hear* them when I peeked at the peeling photograph. So this is the Grandma I would win back from old age and pain; no more blindness from a white blanket of cataracts, no more arthritis that makes her fingers look all knobby and stiff as wood, makes her back and legs seize up and cock her forward so she stoops and shuffles. I know I will find the magic someday, as long as I don't give up hope and stop looking for it. But it's hard sometimes, and soon I will be twelve.

I read a lot, more than anyone else I know, which is probably why I have to wear glasses even though I'm still a girl. The frames are black and shaped like wings, and make my eyes look big and watery like black ponds. I've been reading about orphans lately, books like *Oliver Twist* and *Jane Eyre*. They're always English, it seems, and never Winnebago like me. Grandma Lizzie is from Wisconsin Dells and says that is where our people are from, going way back, but she's lived in Chicago for most of her life, and I've lived here forever. I was born in a stalled car that got stuck in a blizzard on Lake Shore Drive. My dad was trying his best to get Mom to a hospital— he'd borrowed the car—but a snowstorm fell on the city and covered it so quickly people were stuck in their cars and offices and homes, and even in stores and theaters. And it must have felt like another kind of magic—the scary kind where you realize that people are not in charge the way we think we are;

there are spirits that can smother our cities or shake them loose, or shoot at us with lightning cannons in the sky. So I was a small blue icicle-Popsicle baby born in an old Ford—a car that brought life. And it was to be a car that snatched lives away from me too, like it all had to balance out in the end, the giving and taking. My parents were killed in a car accident everyone later blamed on a Wisconsin fog. They'd been to a powwow in Black River Falls, leaving me with Grandma since I was just a baby sick with a flu. That fog confused them somehow, until they couldn't tell the road from the tree line, and they ended up driving into a wall of pines. I was too little to cry about it then, and now I never cry about my parents because I don't think of them as dead at all. Grandma Lizzie and I have been to powwows in Wisconsin and, riding in the backseat of cars, we've been through some of those same smoky fogs, and twice I've seen deer step out of the steamy clouds to stare at us, at our muffled lights. And I've thought that that's what my parents are doing now, wandering the roads as bold, graceful deer, shredding the fog with their antlers, looking for me and looking for me because they love me.

Every day before I walk to school, I comb Grandma Lizzie's hair and make sure her clothes are tidy. She looks old, so old, even though she doesn't have many wrinkles, and she appears angry all the time, grumpy, since her body aches and pinches. She has silver-gray hair, the color of the shiny new double-decker I.C. trains, and she keeps it short, in what she calls a "pixie cut." Grandma doesn't wear any of those fragrances that come out of a bottle, and she's clean as rain, but there's an old lady smell that covers her, trails her, sweet like cough syrup, thick and dank like rotting leaves. I guess I wear her scent on me, too, according to some of the kids at school, especially big-mouthed Tracy Martin who calls me "Grandma Stinky," instead of my true name: Fawn. At lunchtime she wrinkles her nose when I walk past her table in the cafeteria and says, "I smell Grandma Stinky. Eeuuww, she's gonna ruin my lunch with her stink!" She has such a little bitty nose in her pink face I marvel she can catch a whiff of anything at all, let alone me, just minding my own business, lunch bag in one hand and book in the other. Sometimes she'll leave her own food, a thermos of alphabet soup, a carton of chocolate milk, cookies, and a sandwich with the crusts all cut off the white Wonder Bread, and she'll come to my table when I sit by myself, and stand and look over my shoulder. She never touches me or my food, but she likes to tell everybody else what I've packed in my paper sack—most often a small box of dry cereal and a piece of fruit with spots and bruises, like a brown banana, cheaper since we bought it off the sales cart.

When Tracy makes fun of my lunch, I never feel bad on my own account, though to be honest I'd like to mush the banana in her face. Instead I want to cry for Grandma Lizzie, who spends hours every day beading earrings and bracelets and barrettes we will sell at powwows, even though the needlework hurts her hands and takes so much time because she can't see what she is doing. I've separated the tiny cut beads by color and placed them in different bowls in a certain order she has memorized. So she does it all by feel and imagination, making sparkling jewelry in her endless dark. She refuses to apply for Welfare or food stamps, which is why we eat worse than mice and all my clothes hang on me like I'm a broomstick girl with great ugly doorknobs for knees, and wool knee socks that slide down my skinny legs and won't stay up. I want to yell at Tracy: "My grandma does the best she can, so you just shut up! Shut up before I hurt you!" But I never say these things. I just open my book to wherever I left off, and read and read, ferociously, desperately.

It's mainly the white kids who are mean to me and say stupid things; the other Indian kids in my grade will stand up for me if it looks like someone's going to push me around or beat me up, but they don't like me either since I'm always lost in a book rather than playing softball or basketball, or smoking cigarettes behind the gym. They pretty much ignore me unless I get in real trouble. I long to be friends with Gladys Green Deer, or Glad Bags, as her buddies call her. She is tall and beautiful, especially when I've seen her at powwows wearing her traditional Winnebago ribbon-work dress, and beaded moccasins that have pointy toes and a flap folded over the arches. Her earlobes are crowded with long silver earrings, and the eagle feather she pins in her hair is perfect and straight. She is so neat, so pretty, she almost doesn't look real, but more like a character set loose from one of my books. At school she just wears jeans, and her hair is loose rather than arranged in one thick braid, but she's still lovely, and graceful on the basketball court. She can blow perfect smoke rings with her Lucky Strikes, and swear harder than any of the boys. She can pin a girl to the ground in two or three seconds flat, something she's done to Tracy on several occasions, and she speaks fluent Ho Chunk just like me, the language of our tribesmen and ancestors. I want to be friends with Gladys, but I can tell I bore her. I never know what to say when she calls out a greeting. I just duck my head in a nod and smile.

Nearly every weekend there's a powwow at the American Indian Center, a huge old building on Wilson Avenue that used to be a Masonic lodge, so it's full of secret passageways and hidden rooms. Most times we dance in the gym that is also a theater with a stage set against the eastern wall. Opposite the stage, overlooking the enormous, high-ceilinged room, is a balcony the director always keeps locked. I've never been up there myself, even though I've been coming to the Center my whole life. There's an odd thing about the balcony that kids before me discovered: If you knock on the bolted door that leads to the second-floor perch, then press your ear against the rough wood and wait a few seconds, you'll hear a stirring and thumping, like a person roused to his feet, approaching the stairs that lead to the door and your straining ear. The noises aren't loud or obvious, and it can be hard to catch them at all over the music and pounding drum, but there is always a response, never just a silence in answer to a knock. The night watchman has seen strange flashing lights and disappearing figures, so we are all convinced the building is haunted.

The night of the Center Halloween party Grandma Lizzie has dressed like a cat in a fuzzy black sweater and a headband I rigged up with black pipe cleaners to make it look like she has pointy cat ears rising from her head. I drew whiskers and a black nose on her face with a kohl makeup pencil I borrowed from one of her old lady friends who has no eyebrows and paints them on each day.

"How do I look?" Grandma Lizzie asks me before we head out to catch our bus to the Indian Center. Grandma wriggles her nose like a rabbit.

"Well, you *look* like a cat, but you're not acting like one," I scold her.

"Okay, how's this?" Grandma pretends to lick her hand and wash behind the stand-up wire ears. Then she rubs her chin against the doorframe.

"Better, much better."

"Okay, Your Highness, let's get this show on the road."

Grandma can't see my outfit, but I've told her how I made myself a crown out of cardboard and glitter. She let me borrow one of her gauzy party dresses from another time, one that falls to my ankles and almost hides my scuffed loafers. So here I am, transformed into a princess with eyeglasses and long black hair. I am the Princess Fawn.

At the party I eat so much candy—Indian corn and Milk Duds and Three Musketeers bars—I feel queasy and can't dance anymore. I see Gladys and a few of her friends clustered around the door to the balcony, ears against its surface. Clearly they've been trying to summon the ghost. I edge toward them, acting casual, but am nearly trampled in the stampede once they hear the faint noises on the other side. Lanky Winnebago and Chippewa girls gallop away from the balcony door like skittish colts bolting in a storm. They crash into me and drag me along with them, like a fish snagged in their net. We run out of the Indian Center, escaping through the doors on the western side of the building, where there are steps with handrails we like to slide down. Gladys is in charge, as usual, pacing, musing aloud about who the ghost could be.

"Do you think it's one of those old Masons who broke some kind of trust so they walled him up in there and starved him to death? Or is it Vivian's son who died that time from sniffing glue?"

There is a chatter of voices as girls pipe up with their suggestions. I hear a soft low voice that is quieter than the others but more confident, measured, and it takes me by surprise to realize this is my own voice wedging itself into their circle.

"This isn't just a ghost story," I'm telling the girls, "it's also a romantic one. A story of hillbilly love."

"*Hill*billy *love*," Gladys snorts with contempt. "How do you figure *that* happened?" She isn't just poking fun at my opening line, she's curious, too, I can tell. So I find the courage to continue.

I invent a story I have no idea was cooking inside me. This is what I tell them: "A few years back there was a girl named Ronnie, who was sixteen years old and had just moved here with her family from the Appalachian Mountains southeast of here. She had some cousins in Uptown and they showed her the ropes when she arrived, and took her to the Center for the pinball machines in the basement, and the bingo on Sundays, and the free food at powwows. She met one of those Fun Maker boys from the Dells, you know how tall and handsome they are? Well, she met one of them, Kunu, and fell madly in love with him. The kind of crazy love where you can't eat and you can't sleep and you can hardly even breathe. Ronnie had wavy gold hair that fell to her ankles, long as Rita Coolidge's hair, and big green eyes, and the longest eyelashes, and when she looked up at Kunu a certain way he fell in love, too. You'd think that would be that, except both their parents disapproved of their relationship, hers and his. She decided to turn Indian as much as she could because our ways aren't so different from theirs, but there were just a lot of things she didn't know, such as the drum being off-limits to women, being an energy she shouldn't mess with. She loved to hear Kunu sit in at the drum with his uncles and brothers and cousins, and sing so high and so hard. She would stand behind him and lean forward to hear his voice untangled from the rest. And one time, at a Center powwow, after everybody was in line getting their dinner, she knelt down to touch the drum and, more than that, she kissed the spot on the hide that was faded, the decorative paint rubbed off from the pounding of Kunu's drumstick. Nobody saw her do it, nobody was paying any attention to her, but later she told Kunu she'd kissed his drum to show her devotion, and it was only then she learned what a dangerous thing she had done. Kunu wouldn't kiss her good night after the dance, he just left with his family, and she sat outside the Center on these steps, her head on her arms, crying and crying because she hadn't meant to break a taboo and anger the love of her life. She had nearly cried herself out when she felt warm breath on her neck that chilled her and excited her at the same time. He must have come back, she was thinking, and lifted her head to see if it was really Kunu there beside her. But she couldn't see *any*thing, *any*one, just felt the warm wet breath, and then a sucking mouth that slipped from the back of her neck to the side, where her pulsing artery fluttered beneath her skin. The entire neighborhood heard a horrible scream and then dead silence, and it was so awful, dozens of people called the police. They found her in the moonlight, laid out on these steps with her hair running every which way like melted gold. Her green eyes were bulging, staring at the sky, and several policemen slipped on the steps because they were so slick with blood from the wound at her throat where a vengeful spirit had torn it out, her life along with it. My grandma taught me you have to be careful not to anger the spirits or they will punish you in terrible ways. Ronnie's ghost could probably move on if she wanted, but she stays here, looking for Kunu, waiting for him to join her. That's why he doesn't come around the Center so much anymore. He's probably afraid she'll come after him just like the spirit came after her, and eat him, too, like a wolf. She lives up on that balcony and hangs over the edge, tears falling on us, and whenever we knock on her door she starts down, full of hope and dread at the same time—hopeful it will be her love, afraid it will just be us kids."

I stopped talking and found myself the center of attention, an awed silence wrapped around me like one of Grandma Lizzie's old blankets.

"Ronnie, huh?" Gladys finally said. "Not too bad, Fawn. I liked your story."

I have friends now, Gladys Green Deer and her crowd, and Tracy Martin still calls me names, but it doesn't bother me anymore. Even the newest taunt, "Roach Girl," can't bring me down. It's true that Grandma Lizzie and I have a cockroach problem—those little suckers are fearless and determined, and no matter how many Roach Motels I set up to trap them, there's always another crew to replace the last. What they feed on I don't know, since we never have much in the way of groceries, and what we *do* have we keep in the refrigerator, but they share our space undiscouraged by the slim pickings we have to offer. I snap out my clothes before dressing to make sure I'm insect-free when I leave our place, but the other day I forgot, and there I was, walking past Tracy, when one little specimen scuttled from the breast pocket of my dress and made her scream.

"*Ugh!* You disgusting thing!" she shouted at me. "Roach Girl. Roach Girl. Look out for the incredible Roach Girl!"

My Indian friends just shrugged their shoulders because they fight the same battle I do with the bugs and rodents, so it wasn't like news. When I am a princess, I will, of course, have exterminators, so this will no longer be a problem.

I go to sleepover parties at Gladys's place, where we watch Creature Feature horror movies and eat this cool new cereal called Count Chocula. I tell the girls stories before we fall asleep, and no one thinks I'm boring anymore. But some of the stories I keep for myself—like the actual version regarding the ghost in the balcony. I have my own secret idea that Ronnie is just a fiction my imagination pumped into my head. She never really existed beyond my words. I don't think there is only one ghost living behind the balcony door, but two. And they are beautiful spirits surrounded by fog, come to the end of a journey traveled gracefully by night on the roads and highways that lead from Black River Falls to Chicago. And the noises we hear are their hooves and their antlers, because this time they have come back as deer, their eyes as black and watery as my own appear behind the glasses I wear. I believe my parents have found me in Chicago, in this Uptown neighborhood where I live with Grandma. They looked for me and looked for me, because they love me. I believe in them and magic and miracles, and it is all a little easier to have faith in now that I am twelve.

YIDDISCHE BABY

Rivka Galchen

The first time that Uncle Shai came to visit us he drove down to Dallas and bought hundreds of pairs of used blue jeans. He said he had a friend there, another Israeli, who had found the deal. When we laid out those jeans of his all over the living room, my mom called out from the kitchen that the house smelled like the Salvation Army. I told Uncle Shai it was a good smell, but he told me not to worry. He let me help divide the jeans into piles by sizes. "Beautiful!" he exclaimed in Hebrew, pinching my arm. We folded and stacked the jeans, then began tying up the piles with twine.

This was in the 1980s, I was in third grade then, learning about the Oklahoma Land Run and when "i" came before "e," things Uncle Shai knew nothing about. I asked him what he was going to do with all those jeans.

In Israel, he told me, he could sell them for eighty dollars a pair. He didn't have to pause in his tying to speak.

"Even old jeans?"

"*Vintage,*" he said in a throaty English. "They're better than new. They have an American feel."

"Oh," I said.

"Like you," he said.

I asked, "How much did these all cost?"

"Just something—"

"Did you see these holes?"

He stopped tying knots. "People like that, don't they?"

Suddenly I wanted those jeans to make millions. "Oh definitely," I said and began to refold them neatly.

"Yes *definitely*," he agreed, using my word.

When he went to the kitchen, I followed him. He took a potato out of the oven, rinsed it in cold water, and bit into it like an apple. I could see his undershirt through his thin, short-sleeve button-up.

This man—I kept thinking—he's *related* to me.

On his forearms Uncle Shai had wild dark hair, which made me think of Esau, whose mother loved him less than she loved Jacob. Shai spoke to me in Hebrew and when he did speak English he sounded like my dad. Naturally I attached myself to him for his entire visit. Though he was older than my parents, he was also faster and it seemed like I could hear the ticking of his watch from across a room.

Shai let me come along with him on his errands. We drove by winter wheat fields with oil wells; he pulled over and had me take his picture with his heavy, old camera. There was a certain sound of advancing the film, a thin red line that could be seen only through the viewfinder. Then at the Wal-Mart in Sapulpa he filled a cart with deodorants and toothpastes and bath towels, telling me they were gifts for relatives. In Israel, he told me, Ban Roll-On costs ten dollars. In Israel, stores kept toothpaste behind glass cases.

When he said that, I thought of our bathroom closet: we had some fifty boxed tubes of Colgate that my mom had bought on closeout years before. I used to enjoy rearranging the way they were stacked. Sometimes I'd pass time just staring at them and their strange plenty.

After Wal-Mart we went to the grocery store where Shai marveled at the beef. Some cuts were an inch thick and the price per pound was just $1.39. "I'd give up my spleen for this," he said. Somehow I knew what he meant.

As soon as we'd come home from our shopping trips Uncle

Shai would again put a potato in the oven. As we were setting the table for dinner, he'd eat the potato, skin and all, even if it hadn't had time to become tender. His potatoes struck me as biblical and stately. And if I didn't finish my meatballs, say, Shai would look at my plate: "Are you done?" Then he'd eat my leftovers.

One night during dessert, when my dad bragged to Shai about how much I loved school, especially math, Shai grabbed my elbow with his hairy-knuckled, strong hand. "Don't get distracted by boys, Maya-*le*," he said earnestly. "You must be a smart girl and if you study hard, you can be an engineer."

* * *

Shai was my mom's uncle, on her mother's side. He managed her apartment building in Israel, a property she had inherited from a grandfather on her father's side. Any time something went wrong with the building, Shai would call us collect and we'd say that we didn't accept the charges. That was the signal for us to call him back. It all worked out cheaper that way, was my understanding.

"Tell Ema to call me!" Shai would shout recklessly over the pleasant, rote inquiry of the operator. "It's very important!"

Uncle Shai's insufficiently devious collect calls made me tense. I couldn't believe we'd get away with them and sometimes, for fear of breaking the rules, I'd accept them, which inevitably irritated my mom. (And, I assume, Shai.) She would tell me I was a child, which was confusing, since I was, yet I felt I was the one who knew how to behave correctly. Sometimes I pictured my parents at a White House dinner, making too much noise during the soup course. This was before I'd been to Israel enough times, before I thought about how the coiled phone cord looked like the *peises* on the religious men, before I understood that my parents were actually *from* somewhere, not purely eccentricities of their own invention.

My mom, with a sigh, would call Shai back and Shai, according to her, always began with the same first line:

"God Bless you that you don't know—"

After six or seven expensive minutes ("It's terrible! I can't tell you!"), Uncle Shai, with my mom's guidance ("I can't wait until the Messiah,") would diminishingly wind his way to the point.

"It's those ignoramuses in two-B and they didn't tell me— their faucet's been leaking nonstop for days!"

My mom would write this down with a pencil on a random page of the phone directory. "In two-B?"

"In two-B," he would affirm mournfully. As if the faucet were a story so sad as to belong in the newspaper.

My mom had grown fond of saying that Shai cost her more in long distance than he was worth.

Besides the building, we had his jewelry also, my great-grandfather's. It was Turkish gold. The rings were all too big for my mother so she put one on a necklace and wore it like a pendant, which made it seem like someone dear had died. Which, I now understand, was true. The rest of the gold we kept in our freezer, in a plastic bag. For safekeeping? For something.

All these possessions of my great-grandfather's seemed to me a numinous presence amidst our Oklahoman flat foreverness. That building, that gold—it seemed like a phone call from the dead. But why call us? What was there, really, to say?

*　*　*

Managing the property wasn't a full-time job, or at least it shouldn't have been. The building had just eleven apartments and since most of them were still under rent control, tenants almost never moved out. But being overseer of the building was, I began to get the sense, Shai's most reliable and respectable job. Shai regularly insisted that the building was an aging disaster, its plaster an embarrassment, and that if my mom wanted to do things right, she needed to come back to the building, to Israel. He claimed that long distance she would never understand.

"He annoys me," my mom once said. "Don't listen to him, Maya-*le*. He's just an ordinary *schlemiel* and don't imagine he is more than that. He's from an old generation in Israel and they don't make his type anymore, thank God."

But Shai had my heart. At the end of shouting inconsequential disasters to my mother, he took to asking to talk to me. "How's my *malka*?" he'd say. My princess. "How's my beautiful engineer?" "Good!" he'd yell after I answered. Then, accusingly, "You don't have a boyfriend, do you?...Good!" And finally, "It's expensive, so bye!" And he'd hang up the phone before I could say bye back. Talking to him had a deeply familiar feel to it. Like an old pair of jeans.

And, outside of my immediate family, Shai was the only other Jew I really knew. Without realizing it, I had quietly foisted upon him some mysterious, unwieldy hope—some shopping cart overloaded with details of my life. When my dad's father had died, we, unreligious, had spent the next year traveling the hour and a half every Friday to the synagogue in Tulsa to say kaddish. We also drove long distances just to buy halvah, canned poppy seed, the right kind of sardines; in our kitchen we kept a short-wave radio for listening to broadcasts from Israel that we could barely hear. And we talked about money, openly. To spend it on a soda at the movies was unthinkable. We needed to keep it safe and ready for all the inevitable unforeseeable disasters that lay before us.

And there were other little things about my family that I intuited only Shai could decipher or treasure: hammering joyfully on cuts of beef to tenderize them, swishing salt water when I had canker sores. My life had a certain feel to it that I wanted someone, besides me, to love.

With the unquenchable interest one can have in one's self when you think it's not an interest in yourself, I tried to learn about Uncle Shai. I discovered only an outline. My mother told me that as far as she knew her uncle had come to Israel from Syria, as a teenager, with no parents, and that he had always cast about from venture to venture, trying to make money and never succeeding. Besides jeans, he had imported shoes, washing machines, women's underwear. He'd been hit over the head with a bat by loan sharks. For a spell he'd organized jeep tours for tourists, but then came the Yom Kippur war, during which Shai served at a postal station because he could read many alphabets. He had married late in life because he had thought he would one day be able to get a degree first, which he never was able to do, and his wife died early on of stomach cancer. Shai had one child, a son, Eli. Eli was studying to be an engineer.

* * *

One day, when I was about fifteen, the kitchen phone rang. My mom answered and it was Shai, but it was not a collect call. I mostly heard just one side of the conversation, but I know it began: "God Bless you that you don't know."

My mom was twirling the phone cord idly. "Tell me, Shai." She sighed. He must have answered quietly, because normally I could hear the commotion of his anxiety from across the room.

Abruptly, my mom stopped swinging the phone cord. "What?" I still couldn't hear what Shai was telling her, just my mom's punctuation of what he said: "That's terrible!" She let the phone cord hang limply, drag on the ground. "You should have called earlier—" She drew closer to the base of the phone. When my dad wandered into the kitchen, my mom held her hand up to silence him before he could say anything. He shrugged and turned to open the refrigerator. I was wondering when Uncle Shai would ask to talk to me. But also I remember a klunky, disjointed sensation, a knowing that the flat awkward moment, like the sound of the refrigerator door closing, was going to stick in my mind.

"We'll pay half the fare!" my mom was shouting into the phone. Then she replaced the receiver slowly.

"Leaky faucet?" my dad asked.

No, she said. Eli, Shai's son, was seeing a *shikse*.

Oh, I thought. Oh no?

My parents communed about this strange fate that had befallen Shai, while I still wondered blankly what *shikse* meant. I had definitely heard the word before but *shikse,* unlike *meshugge* or *schlemiel*, had no application in my Oklahoma life. What was the point in having a word that described, well, basically every female I knew? I imagined someone shy, but with a kick to her. Or an older woman who told people to shush. But I knew those guesses were juvenile. Did it mean prostitute? Did it mean lesbian? Hadn't I heard it used in that way?

"What does *shikse* mean?" I finally braved.

My mom slapped me. Then she apologized. She'd never done anything like that before.

*　*　*

A few years earlier, when I was in the sixth grade, after a barrage of collect phone calls, we had flown to Israel. An apartment in our building had been vacated and we stayed there, sleeping on the floor. I remember inspecting every recess, opening each reticent drawer. The small toilet in the bathroom flushed weakly and, to take a warm shower, I had to flip a red switch fifteen minutes ahead of time. When I was done, I had to remember to turn it off so as not to burn out the circuit. The first time I tried to open the windows I had to ask for help, because they worked in a way unfamiliar to me, opening out rather than up. In the living room, the space of a perfectly absent wooden slat stared up from the floor and the three-pronged electricity outlets looked like angry-browed faces. Only the clothesline seemed exciting to me. The wires were on pulleys and hanging out your pants to dry felt like a message to the world.

In the mornings we worked on repairs. The place did need attention. "Was I right?" Shai said.

"It crumbles just as well while we're here," my mother had answered, kind of joyfully.

Later my mom, my dad, and I went into narrow stores and argued with men about caulking. My mother, it turned out, could retile a shower. She could fix leaky faucets. She could even repair a gas stove. She said she remembered when her family had bought a similar stove, when she was a girl. She could still picture her grandfather at night, checking, suspiciously, that the gas was really off.

"Okay then," said my father, cutting her off. She kissed him, and grabbed his hand, which made her seem like a stranger to me.

We went for dinner to the home of friends of my parents. I had never thought of my parents as people who had friends. That particular night I remember slicing into a meatball and being startled to find inside a perfectly intact hard-boiled egg. The sliced meatball stared at me with its yellow eye, so I ate it quickly, without taste, to escape its gaze. In the end, the whole trip disoriented me in that simple, complete way. Long meals were new to me—and there were so many of them—as were the women with bold eye make-up and wiry brown husbands. I remember falling asleep on blocky sofa cushions, people I didn't know petting my hair gently, distractedly, as if I were familiar. Eventually, still half-asleep, my dad would carry me out to the car. On the drive back to the apartment we'd pass almost no streetlights, so the only moment that would wake me would be the end: the unclicking of seatbelts, the sigh of opened doors.

Each time we would again arrive at our ghostly apartment building, the idea that we were connected to it again startled me. The building itself seemed alien, with its nubbly exterior, its timed stairwell lights that always clicked themselves off before I got to the top of the stairs. I couldn't imagine us owning any building at all, and certainly not this one that seemed so indifferent. And yet the building had a feel to it all the same, something familiar. I came to think of it like a garbled news report on a short-wave radio that I imagined I understood. The angry-face outlet plates, the finicky shower, they came, eventually, to seem to me like eccentric relatives, like keys to myself.

Supposedly we had come to Israel expressly to renovate and rent that apartment. However, so far as I understood, we received very little in earnings from the building and any money we did make had gone, for years, into a bank account in Israel. Exchanging shekels for dollars meant paying a large tax, but apparently most Israelis evaded this problem in the same way.

We visited a little raven of a religious man and sat around a small coffee table protected by a lace tablecloth. The old man set out plates of wafer cookies and a bowl of dates. He poured fragrant coffee for all of us. I put in three sugar cubes and then drank mine in counted sips; it was in a lovely, tiny-flowered cup.

I came to understand that this man was exchanging our shekels for dollars, and that this was all being done on what was called the black market. The adults counted and recounted. I ran my finger across the bumps of the lace tablecloth. In the end it was Shai, with his efficient hairy knuckles, who dexterously collected the bills into bundles and bound them with thick strips of newsprint paper.

Afterward we went and bought toothpaste for me. I loved the toothpaste in Israel because it came in flavors other than mint. I bought a dozen tubes of the orange-flavored kind. The tubes weren't plastic like at home, but rather a durable metal.

"It's not so black, the black market," Shai reassured me when I asked a short time later as we sat in the bright sun at a falafel stand, eating pickles and falafel.

My mom offered casually, "Black market rates are published in the newspaper." My dad wasn't even listening. He had gone back to put more shredded cabbage and fried eggplant on his plate. "The government publishes them," my mom continued. My dad came back to the table with his pita, with extra napkins and an orange Fanta with a straw.

At home, my dad asked me questions like, "Do you say 'chill down' or 'chill out'?" My mom made me do the talking when we ordered pizza. It struck me that, in Israel, my parents made sense, had grace.

When we boarded the airplane for home my mom had cash in a pouch taped around her stomach, a loose sweater pulled over on top. We didn't declare this on the customs form that I read over and over again with reluctant elation. Uncle Shai, I kept thinking, he knew this about us, he knew everything. My mother's sweater was orange and at the cuffs the sleeves were fluffy. I wanted to put my hand on her stomach, like she was pregnant.

*   *   *

A week after the non-collect phone call Shai showed up at our doorstep with Eli at his side. Eli looked like Uncle Shai but less hairy. He wore blue jeans. A thin gold chain decorated his neck. He gave me a disinterested smile, then checked his watch. My mom descended on Eli with compliments and led him into the kitchen where she began to heat up rice with lentils. Over the anonymous whir of the microwave I heard: "Look how great you look, you could have any girl that you want!"

It struck me then that my mom was off-key, uncorrectable.

I had prepared a potato for Shai, and offered it to him, but he said he would save his appetite for later. "How's my *malka*?" he asked me, laying his hand on my head, and I really could hear the ticking of his watch. "How's my engineer?...you're so tall...you don't have a boyfriend, do you?"

With a concentrated offhandedness, I said, No.

"Good!" he said. Then he asked me if I knew trigonometry. He wrote down a math problem, and sent me off, bidding me to solve it. I didn't find that strange.

•

I'd been told we had an emergency on our hands. Shai and Eli were to stay for three months. My dad had arranged for Eli to have a job delivering for the Pizza Shuttle. We loaned him a car for that. My mom had bought new bedding and made the converted garage into a respectable room for Eli. Shai would be sleeping in the living room. Both were to share a bathroom with me.

"How would you feel if your boyfriend was away for three months?" Shai said to me the first night, as we were brushing our teeth. I shrugged my shoulders uncomfortably.

Then Eli appeared at the door.

Shai spat. "Isn't this boy beautiful?" he said to me. "He's my life."

Eli said nothing but brushed his teeth. Shai stuck around with a towel at his neck, leaning too close into the mirror, flossing.

Eventually the bathroom became just mine and Eli's. Shai, busy walking the neighborhood, went to bed much later than us. Eli often brushed his teeth for what seemed like a full minute, which shamed me into doing the same. We'd leave the water running the whole time, something that Shai had told me was a very American thing to do. Eli would spit, then catch running water in his cupped hand. I had a little small glass for getting my water. I offered to get Eli one but he said, "No thanks, beauty."

Eli was related to me and I knew I wasn't supposed to fall in love with him. Also he was twenty-one and I was fifteen. But we became friends, slowly. I told him about my crush, my lab partner in biology whose legs stretched long under our shared table. Eli asked me, of him, if he mixed meat and milk. I didn't understand his joke.

Early in the mornings, before I would leave for school, Eli would come into my room to borrow the phone. As far from the door as possible, he'd lie on the carpet on his stomach with the cord stretched across my bed, while I went out to the kitchen to eat my sunny-side-up eggs and talk to my mother animatedly, as if running distraction.

Eli must have spent all his pizza money on long distance.

He had shown me a picture of the "*shikse.*" She had long thick dark curls and wore jeans and a white shirt with belled sleeves; she was pretty enough. She kind of looked like me, as if she was a cousin, though I knew obviously that she wasn't. Her name was Reem and she was Lebanese. She and Eli were students together at the university.

"What does she study?" I asked because I didn't feel I was allowed to ask anything else.

"Engineering."

At my school, in History period, I had learned the story of the famous Cherokee, Elias Boudinot. He had fallen in love with a white woman whose father had reluctantly agreed to the marriage but insisted that it be kept secret. The citizens had found out and burnt the woman in effigy in the town square. I had to explain to Eli what "effigy" meant. It meant they didn't really burn her. I assured him that, in the end, the couple ran away from town and lived happily ever after. Boudinot became a big man in politics. He started the first Cherokee press.

"Thanks, Maya. That's an idiotic story," Eli said. "Why are you telling me this?"

"I'm just telling you," I said.

"My dad's not as ridiculous as you think."

Shai also borrowed my phone once and, standing the whole time, shouted. The phone cord quivered. Very biblically, earnestly. I was mad at Shai, and felt superior to him, and felt guilty about being mad and feeling superior, so I went and leaned against him and he put his arm around me. I could hear his heart thumping, this beautiful full sound. "Don't do anything until I come back," he called into the phone angrily. He told me the phone call was about some neighborhood kids who had, with rocks, broken two of the windows of the apartment building. He kissed me on the forehead and told me to go study.

The following Saturday morning Shai sat me down with great formality. "*Malka*," he said to me, his brown eyes wet. "We've been here for a few weeks now." I found myself looking at the thready pulse of his wrist, but then looked back up at his face. "Don't you have any nice Jewish girls to introduce to Eli?" He was holding my elbow. His hand wasn't soft. Looking at his shoulder to avoid his gaze, I could see the silhouette of his undershirt, the hair at his collar.

I felt like a terrible failure.

I didn't know how to tell him, to remind him, that not only was I much younger than Eli, but also that he and Shai were basically the only other Jews that I knew.

Shai didn't understand, really, where we were, what that meant. "How can you not know any Jews?" To Shai, to all our Israeli relatives, the United States was basically New York, Florida, and California; he didn't understand that Oklahoma was not part of any of those states, but rather its own place altogether. "Not many Jews, I'll grant you," he said, "but are you going to tell me that there's not a single Jewish girl you can introduce Eli to?" Yes, I said, I was going to tell him that. "Do you hate me? Bring me the phone book." He found no Rubin. He found no Cohen. "But look here Maya," he said, "Who is this C. Levine? He must have children. Who is he?" And I actually did know who was listed under Levine because he was my piano teacher. He'd had, supposedly, a Jewish great-grandfather, a traveling merchant who had married a beautiful Cherokee, that was the story.

"A dog deserves better," I overheard Shai saying as I pulled a pair of shrunken jeans from the dryer later that day. I went to my room and tried stretching the jeans out again by putting them on. I managed to get them on, but they were so tight that my stomach hurt. Just sitting down in a chair was difficult.

"*Motik*," my mom said, when I went to her for advice "You look like you're selling yourself, you can't wear those jeans." That was how my mom talked. Sometimes it upset me, but usually it impressed me. I almost wanted to tell her what Shai had said to me, wanted to hear her laugh, wanted to be reassured that she would laugh.

But then at dinner: "She just didn't want a *yiddische* baby," Shai was explaining.

"Yes," my mom agreed. "I saw that."

"Not that she wasn't a good girl—" Shai amended.

"Oh yeah, I definitely liked her—" my mom added. They were discussing a certain Nicole, who had married Shai's cousin Nomi. Nicole, a *shikse* obviously, had met Nomi at UC San Diego. They had never been able to conceive. Eventually Nicole left Nomi, Nomi still gave her money mind you, and now Nicole had had a baby with someone else. "But if someone doesn't want a *yiddische* baby, then they won't have a *yiddische* baby," my mother trailed off before returning to her chicken.

"I *knew* that was why she couldn't get pregnant," Shai proclaimed. "I knew from the beginning."

A chewing pause ensued before Eli decided to add: "Nice to dine with Einsteins."

I was too slow to get in a word.

"Eli, you met Nicole, didn't you?" Shai said, accusingly. "You thought she was pretty."

Eli ignored his father.

Shai went on: "Well, I certainly thought she was pretty. You should see the baby," he said looking at my mom, "the baby she had with this other man, a Californian—a beautiful baby!"

My mom caressed the ring pendant on her necklace. She was ignoring Shai, but only because she was still focused on

Eli. She looked straight at him. "Nomi's all alone now," she said. "He pays alimony and drives a cab."

"Nomi never sticks with anything," my dad said, "He probably drove that girl away with his this and his that and the other—"

"That's what I think too!" I said.

Then everyone at the table, even Eli, looked at me, like I was the stupidest person they had ever met. My dad touched my elbow and whispered loudly, "Just so you know, Maya, if you ever get married in a church, I won't be there."

Oh. Eli stood up. His chair, in its moving, screeched against the floor. He opened his mouth but said nothing. He closed it and walked measuredly into the kitchen. Then he walked past us all again, carrying a bowl of steamed potatoes back to his bedroom in the garage. He didn't slam the door; his not doing that was somehow very spiteful, and serious.

Shai told Eli that it was not polite for a guest to tie up the phone line.

"Primitive!" Eli shouted through the door.

"You don't understand history!" Shai called out, his face red. "It's fine with you if our suffering was for nothing!"

I saw Eli walk out across the front lawn, a shade in the dusk. Later I went outside and sat against the outside door to the garage and did my homework there, under the security light. I felt the absence of Eli on the other side of the door, as obvious as a missing slat in a wood floor.

The evening was warm and across the way, near the creek, I could see the silent fireflies. The Oklahoma spring smell, of still warm sod, hung heavily. A moth fell stunned onto my notebook, then fluttered away. What, I wondered, really was a *shikse*? Wasn't it just someone who didn't have that *yiddische* feel to her? Someone with different plates covering her electricity outlets? Someone surprised to find an egg inside her meatball? Wasn't a *shikse* simply someone who was not like Shai, not like my parents, not even like Reem, but more like me?

* * *

One time when we were visiting Israel, staying in the apartment building, I didn't properly secure my clothing when I hung it on the clothesline. I leaned out the window that evening to gather my week's worth of wash, only to discover that it had all blown away. The barren metal wires, trembling in the breeze, squeaked their innocence. I spotted only one T-shirt, amidst the distant branches of an unsurprised urban tree. My jeans, my shirts, my socks: they were nowhere to be seen.

This was a couple of years after Eli and Shai's visit. Eli and Reem had married hastily in Cyprus and now had a baby.

I was seventeen by this time, too conscious of the distance between who I was and who I wanted to be; I could feel the gap like a constant chill. Odd as it sounds, hanging my clothes out to dry, rather than tossing them into a machine, was a great pleasure for me. When I'd bring my clothes in off the line they had the crispness and scent of the greater world. Or that's how I felt at the time.

Since we were staying in Israel all summer my mom drove me out to the Dizengoff shopping center to look for new clothes. Together we picked out two boatneck tops, a denim skirt, and a tank dress, all in styles popular there at that time. The outfits were more playful, maybe sexier than the outfits girls were wearing back home. We also bought socks and underwear, and even those items were different. The underwear was more utilitarian, no bows, no lace. The socks were slippery and elegant.

Later that day, from a distance I caught sight of myself in a mirror, wearing one of the new boatneck shirts. I didn't recognize myself at first. The mirror formed the back wall of a narrow gyros restaurant and the reflection, meant to make a small place feel spacious, could catch you by surprise, startle you. I saw a girl who looked wiry, tan, feminine. She looked like a local.

When I recognized her as me, she seemed to fade and flatten. I had an overwhelming sense of some other person I could have been, but wasn't. I had lost her. I felt pulseless, transparent.

We were just sitting there, my mom and I, eating. Not really talking. Avoiding the mirror, I stared dully at that gold ring my mom wore as her necklace. I idly shifted lentils around on my plate. Eventually, of course, I looked over at the boys, men really, who worked behind the counter. One boy wore a fitted plain white T-shirt. He had strong arms, a short haircut—probably he was still a soldier. He was buttering sheets of phyllo dough. He was so beautiful.

If I were a real Israeli girl, I thought, I'd have something to say to him. I'd say something to him and he'd say something to me and any time I'd come back we'd banter a moment and it would all be nothing and yet also the finest thing.

He caught me staring at him, smiled briefly and went on with his work. He didn't blush, as I would have, or sweat. Normally, I hardly had the courage to look, let alone to be looked at. Though occasionally, some strange thing inside me would make me reach out and, uninvited, touch a boy's face.

When I reached the apartment that evening, when I ran up the stairs quickly, before the automatic hall lights had switched off, I thought to myself that the girl I had seen wasn't just another girl I could have been, a loss, but maybe also the girl that I was. I have to assume it wasn't just the boatneck shirt. We have strange hollows in us that are our very sounds, parts of ourselves, I wanted to believe, more essential and irrefutable than just the small sum of experiences. The startling part for me was that, with time, I began to cherish my unelected characteristics most of all. How ridiculous, how shameful—to cherish what you were more than what you made of yourself. But it seemed, for a time, the least lonely thing to do.

I heard the click-clicking of my father lighting the gas stove, putting on a teakettle. I lay on the sofa, reading Mark Twain, who was floating down a river. The kettle trembled with heat. I had the feeling, that evening, that I understood something of my great-grandfather who had given this building even to me, whom he had never met. He just wanted to live on along with us. It was primitive really, almost biological. He had called— we had come. We wore his jewelry. We would have possessed him anyway, no matter the distance, even if he hadn't called.

THE SUMMER OF ICE CREAM

By Tope Folarin

About a year before the summer of ice cream began, my father called Tayo and me into the living room. He asked us to sit on the couch and, with tears in his eyes, he told us that he would be leaving his job at the Kodak plant in Salt Lake City. Someone had drawn a picture of my father and hung it on the side of his cubicle. His facial features were greatly exaggerated and blood dripped from the nostrils. My father said that they made him look like an evil monkey.

Tayo and I glanced at each other as Dad spoke, and then Tayo stared down at the yellowing carpet. I could not help but shake my head. Though we were both scared, and angry, we weren't really surprised. This was just the latest in a long series of job disappointments.

We knew that things had been easier for Dad once. He had told us how, as a young student in Nigeria almost fifteen years before, he applied to a college in Utah on a whim, and learned shortly afterward that he'd been awarded a full scholarship. How his new school, Davis State University, sponsored his move to Utah, and covered the airfare for his new bride as well. How—unlike almost everyone he knew—he received a visa to travel to the United States on his first try. He had arrived in America believing that his American dream was already coming true.

But his life began to unravel the moment his feet touched American soil. His wife became pregnant, and then she became ill. Mom began to see things that weren't there, to speak with people who did not exist. Dad had to drop out of school to take care of her and his newborn son. Another son soon followed. Dad was then forced to work wherever he could: as a janitor, a street sweeper, and a security guard. At first, each job seemed to present him with an opportunity to move up and make his mark in America, but then he was laid off without explanation or he quit because he was tired of being bullied. My mother returned to Nigeria somewhere in the middle of this, to rest and recover. She promised Tayo and me that when she returned she would be back to her old self. We never saw her again.

I remember how excited Dad was when he was hired by Kodak. The job didn't pay very much, he said, but he would get to wear a suit and tie every day. I was in awe of the idea of my father dressing up to go to work, instead of wearing a drab, gray jumpsuit. The night before his first day, I helped Dad iron his favorite brown suit, the one with the missing top button and the small tear in the middle of the right sleeve. The next morning, I felt so proud of him that I lingered in the car after he pulled up in front of my school, and I smiled at him like my face could do nothing else. Even though I'd spent my entire life in America, at that moment I felt as if we had all just arrived and that everything was about to change.

After leaving Kodak, my father quickly found another job, at Layton Rental. The place was filled with an assortment of machines that could be rented for varying periods of time. Dad seemed happy there, and he always answered the phone when I called: "Hello, Layton Rental. Wale speaking!"

Sometimes I called just to hear his voice. He always sounded cheerful, even if he'd left home carrying sorrow in his eyes.

"Hello, Daddy! Can I have a lawn mower, please?"

"Yes, for how long?"

"I only need it for a couple minutes."

"Okay, that's fourteen million dollars."

"Daddy! I only have seven cents!"

"Okay, I will give you the family discount. We will hold it for you. When are you coming?"

However, after a few months, my father began to come home angry. He told us that his accent was preventing him from getting ahead.

I had never heard him complain about his accent before. I didn't really know what an accent was. I knew Dad's voice was different—he didn't speak like my teachers or my friends—but in my mind the difference was a positive one. His voice sounded royal to me; I thought he had the kind of voice that everyone wanted, a deep, forceful voice that instantly marked him as someone who was important.

Dad felt otherwise. One evening, at the dinner table, he advised Tayo and me in a determined, icy voice: "Look here, be proud that you have an American accent," he said, calmly, icily. "People can say anything they want about the way you look, about your skin. But if you learn to speak better than them, there is *nothing* they can do. They cannot prevent you from moving ahead."

Dad began to make us watch the evening news every night so we'd learn how to speak what he called "professional English." I began to notice the differences.

My father said "chumorrow," and the white, well-coifed hosts said "tomorrow."

"Tomorrow, negotiations begin."

"Tomorrow, the president will meet with the grieving families."

"Tomorrow, the cease-fire goes into effect."

My father said "haboh" instead of "harbor." He said "paloh" instead of "living room."

My second-grade teacher asked me where my homework was the day I forgot to bring it to school.

"I left it in my paloh, on the couch."

"Your *paloh*?"

I looked, confused, at my classmates, who tittered around me. "My paloh. With the TV, couch, rug..."

My teacher smiled. "Oh. You mean your living room. Okay, that's fine. Don't forget to bring it in tomorrow. And try to remember, when you're at school, it's a living room."

I burned with shame, then anger. Years later, I finally figured out that my father was saying "parlor."

On a warm fall Saturday, just a few months after he started working at Layton Rental, my father asked Tayo and me to put on our church clothes and get in the car. We drove swiftly down the shining highway with our windows open, as if through a corridor of wind and gold, and arrived at the Salt Lake City International Airport an hour later. Dad smiled sadly as he left the car, and he told me to move to the backseat. That evening we returned home with a new mother, a tall, beautiful, stately woman we had never seen before. Her two sons came with us. Femi looked a bit younger than Tayo, about seven or so. Ade was two or three.

Just like that, we were a family. The rest of our lives began to happen so quickly that Tayo and I didn't have much of a chance to ask Dad who our new mom was, or how he had met her. We never got to ask him why things had to change.

After resting for a week, my stepmother—Tayo and I called her Mom because Dad insisted—began to leave the house every morning to look for work. She had a nursing degree from a college in Lagos and, in less than two weeks, she found a job at St. Paul's Hospital, the biggest in town. Femi, Tayo, and I soon discovered (by huddling near our parents' bedroom door as they argued quite loudly one evening) that Mom's salary was substantially higher than Dad's. In the days following their argument, my father began to complain even more about Layton Rental.

He began to deliver rousing pep talks to himself at all hours of the day, even when he was driving us to school: "... that is the promise of this country! I must become an entrepreneur! That is my fate in this world! That is why God put me here! I am wasting my talents giving all my skill to these people! That's why I'm not getting ahead! I must take the horn by the bulls!"

He spoke this way for many weeks, but nothing really changed.

A few months later, just after I turned ten, Dad woke me up early on a Saturday morning and told me we had somewhere special to go. He took me to the post-office headquarters in Salt Lake City. We drove around the place until we saw a massive parking lot filled with dozens of gleaming white mail trucks. From afar they looked almost like large immobile sheep.

"My truck is there," he said, pointing toward the lot. "Trust me, Tunde, our lives will be changing very soon."

When I asked him if he planned on becoming a mailman, he smiled but he wouldn't answer. The following week, on the Friday before our last week of school, Dad told my brothers and me about his plan.

"Today, I am beginning my life again," he said. "I've quit my job at Layton Rental. I've purchased an old post-office truck from the government. I will turn it into an ice-cream truck. All of us will have to work together. Since you guys will be out of school for the summer next week, I expect that all of you will come with me when I start. We will have to work hard. If we honor what God has given us, God will honor us even more. Okay? Any questions?"

We shook our heads.

Dad smiled. He looked taller than usual, somehow, and his wide forehead was gleaming.

"Okay! That's all."

The next morning, my father woke us up in his customary way. He stood in the doorway of our bedroom while the sun was still asleep and began to sing.

"Good morning, good morning, it's time to wake up! Good

morning, good morning, it's time to wake up! Doo doo doo! Doo doo doo!"

We groaned as loudly as we could, but Dad simply sang over our complaints. How could someone be so cheery in the morning? It was almost as if he were intentionally torturing us. When he finished singing, Tayo, Femi, and I rolled out of our beds and quickly got ready in the bathroom, all of us in the shower at the same time. When we were dressed, we stood in a line in the living room, as we did every Saturday morning. Dad emerged from his room a few moments later, and he paced up and down the line.

"Are you guys ready?"

"Yes, sir!"

"What are we doing today?"

"Work, sir!"

"And how long will we work?"

"As long as it takes, sir!"

Satisfied, my father strode to the door and walked out, and we followed him.

Outside, we saw an old postal truck and another car he hadn't told us about. Our ancient Chrysler station wagon was gone.

"Surprise!"

We rushed to the car and huddled around it. It was a light-blue Chevy sedan. The paint shimmered in the sunlight; the car looked brand new. We danced around it, and Dad nodded. "I bet you can't guess how much it was," he said, pointing at the car.

We laughed with incomprehension.

"Only five hundred dollars! The government gave me a discounted price because I bought it with the truck. Your daddy knows how to drive a bargain!"

We were already inside the Chevy by then. I was doing some great imaginary driving on an imaginary road, Tayo and Femi pointing out imaginary landmarks as we passed. Dad allowed us to play for a few minutes but then he called us back to the mail truck. He pointed to the truck and we gathered solemnly before it.

"This is our future," he said. "We must respect it."

We knew what he was actually saying; "respect" had mysteriously become a synonym for "clean like crazy" since our stepmother and stepbrothers had arrived from Nigeria. So we trudged into the garage and grabbed a few pails and sponges and followed Dad to the back of the truck. He turned a handle on the bottom of the back door and pushed the door up with both hands. Inside it looked much as I thought it would— big and empty and dirty. There were a few grimy shelves my brothers and I had to take apart and cart into the garage, and a couple registration stickers on the windshield that we couldn't remove despite our best efforts, but we had fun cleaning the floor and walls, occasionally blasting one another with the hose as Dad shouted directions outside.

He inspected the truck when we finished, and after pointing out a few spots that we had supposedly missed, he called us into the Chevy. We drove for about fifteen minutes, past the houses of our neighborhood, then the shuttered neighborhood stores, with their broken windows and façades of peeling paint, and then past Walmart and the colossal Sam's Club that had opened only a few weeks before. He parked in front of a large warehouse with a few trailers outside.

"Tunde, follow me inside. The rest of you, behave while we're gone."

A youngish-looking man with red hair and porcelain skin smiled nervously. "I've been waiting for you guys!" he said as we walked in.

He ushered us to a room in the back and led us to an imposing door at the far end. The man turned a wheel where a doorknob should have been and opened it. The interior exhaled frosty bursts of air all over us. We walked inside, shivering, and saw dozens of boxes piled atop one another. The man gestured to a pile of boxes off to one side.

"There's your order, sir. All the ice cream you asked for should be there."

My ears perked up. Ice cream?

"Thank you, sah."

Dad pointed to the boxes and I picked up a couple and carried them back to the car. "There's more inside," I told my brothers, and they tumbled out of the car to help. By the time we were finished we had filled the trunk and part of the backseat with boxes of ice cream. Dad jumped in and we sped back home. Once there, we carried the boxes to the freezer in the garage. It was an old 1960s-era freezer that made a great deal of noise—sometimes a hacking cough, sometimes a strangling sound—but it was very cold inside. We stacked the boxes neatly without opening them, and we called Dad when we were done.

"Good job," he said. Then he reached into the freezer and pulled a box from the middle. We gathered around him as he opened it, and we saw the tidy packages of ice cream bars stacked in perfect rows. Dad selected a package from the top, and we read the label aloud.

"Choco Taco," we said, in awed unison.

Dad smiled at us. Then he lifted the package to the ceiling and blessed it. He passed a package to each of us, and we sat down in the middle of the garage to consume our treats.

*

On the first day of our summer vacation, Dad drove Tayo and me to the Middleton Junkyard in our new ice-cream truck. He asked the man behind the desk to follow us, and we walked through the industrial rubble until we came upon a long, sleek-looking freezer. Dad pointed at it.

"This is the one I want. How much?"

The man wheezed. "For this? This is top of the line, yes sir. This'll probably run you about . . . oh, I'd say about two hundred fifty dollars."

"But it doesn't work," my father replied flatly.

"Don't matter. She's a looker. I could get someone to come out here and pay three hundred for her."

Back and forth they went until they settled on a price. One hundred eighty-five dollars, and the man threw in a carburetor for free. Dad laughed long and hard after the man left to draw up our receipt.

"See? What did I tell you? I drive the best bargains in all of Utah!"

We returned home with the freezer in the back of the truck, and Femi joined us in cleaning it. When we finished, Dad told us to transfer a few boxes of ice cream from the freezer in the garage to the freezer in the truck. We did as we were told, and then Femi asked him how the ice cream would stay cold since the freezer didn't work. Dad turned around in his seat.

"Why don't you guys trust me? I have everything covered. Are you finished?"

We nodded and Dad immediately put the truck into reverse. We drove only a few minutes, to a small house across the street from Middleton High School. Yellow paint was peeling from the exterior, and the wooden steps leading up to the porch were cracked, but the house still had a solid, dependable aura about it.

"Femi and Tunde, follow me."

Dad knocked on the door and an older man with shoulder-length gray hair opened it. He was wearing a thin, plaid shirt and the top two buttons were undone. His gray chest hairs peeked out at us. Dad smiled and the man smiled back.

"You're . . ."

"Mr. Akinola," Dad said.

"Ah! Nice to meet you. So just one block then?"

"Yes, sah."

"Okay then, follow me."

"Can my children watch?"

"Of course they can. Come on down here, guys!"

We followed Dad and the old man to the basement. It was dim in there, but I could see a small freezer against the far wall, and an ancient-looking upright saw with rust on the blades resting beside it. The old man put on a pair of gloves that were resting on top of the freezer and pulled a steaming block of clouded ice from inside. He placed the ice on a tray that was attached to the saw and pressed a button at the base of it. Then he slid the ice back and forth before the screeching blade; solid slices separated themselves from the block until the block disappeared. The old man deftly wrapped each slice of clouded ice in brown paper, and he placed each slice in a large cardboard box.

"Here you go, sir," he said, handing the box over to Dad. "Remember what I said on the phone. This'll last you a couple days. Gotta treat it carefully. It'll burn you."

Dad turned to us.

"Are you listening to him? Did you hear what he said? I know you guys sometimes like to learn with your hands instead of your ears. If you don't listen, it will be a very painful lesson!"

In the truck, Dad tore the paper off two of the packages and dropped the ice on the boxes in the freezer.

"What's that?" Femi asked.

"Dry ice," Dad said.

"But it will melt all over the ice cream, and the ice cream will get soggy," I said.

"No. It won't melt," Dad said. "It will only evaporate."

I thought he was playing a trick on us. When he turned away, I looked again at the ice in the freezer. Already the entire freezer was filling up with a thick fog. I pressed my finger to the mysterious ice, and a few seconds later I felt a stinging fire flow from the tip of my finger to the top of my arm.

I screamed. Dad whirled around and caught me with my finger on the ice. I couldn't pull it away. He quickly opened a bottle of water that was near the gearshift and poured it over the ice until my finger came loose. I looked at my quivering finger and noticed that my skin had burned away, leaving only a red pulsating sketch of the skin that had once been there.

"What did I tell you about touching that ice, Tunde? What did I tell you?"

I hung my head in shame, as Dad and my brothers laughed at me.

Dad put the rest of the dry ice into the old freezer in the garage when we got home. Then he went inside and emerged a few moments later with a small cardboard box.

"The final step," he said.

He opened the box and pulled out a rectangular device that had two switches on the top and a mess of wires on the bottom. I couldn't read what was written beneath the switches because Dad took the device inside the truck and started working. We saw him battling with wires and pliers; we heard him curse occasionally under his breath. We eventually grew tired of watching him and went inside to watch TV.

Dad strolled into the living room an hour later and told us to come outside. He went in on the driver's side of the truck and clicked something, and we heard a familiar song flowing out of the horn-shaped speaker he'd placed at the front of the truck, just above the windshield.

"That's the ice-cream music!" Tayo cried. We recognized the tune from the ice-cream trucks that we'd seen on TV. We'd never seen an ice-cream truck in Middleton, though.

Dad nodded excitedly. Then we linked arms and listened together.

The following morning Dad woke us up with his good-morning song, and when we reached the garage we saw an old, thin, beat-up mattress on the floor.

"Put it in the back of the truck," he said. "That's where you guys will relax between your shifts."

We placed the mattress where he told us, right up against the freezer, and we brought along a couple of pillows so the bed would be even more comfortable. As we were reclining on it, Dad appeared and stared at us.

"Aren't you forgetting something?"

Tayo, Femi, and I looked at each other, and then we looked around. Dad shook his head slowly.

"What about your books? What do you think this is? A time to rest? If you aren't working, then you're reading! Go bring your books!"

We ran back inside and brought out a couple of books and placed them on the mattress. Dad surveyed the titles and shook his head again.

"Bring more. I expect each of you to finish one book each day."

We brought more books and piled them high against the freezer. Dad nodded, then he settled in the driver's seat and flipped on the music. He began humming to himself as he started the engine. He drove down the length of our street, took a right onto Jones Place, and then he slowed down.

Tayo, Femi, and I were familiar with these streets; we'd spent hours walking around our neighborhood in search of kids who might be interested in playing basketball with us, but our neighborhood looked different, somehow, from the windows of our ice-cream truck. The houses looked the same, like precise replicas of our own house, with their small front lawns and brown-tiled roofs, but now the people we saw walking their dogs and kicking soccer balls were no longer friends, or even neighbors—they were all potential customers. A few people simply stared at our truck as we passed. Most of the people we saw ignored us completely. On two occasions, we saw a child looking expectantly in our direction, and we yelled at Dad to stop. Dad listened and pulled the truck over to the curb, but both times the child shyly waved at us and ran away. We continued searching for customers, but after we'd been on the road for an hour or so my brothers settled down in the back to read. Dad asked me to sit on the chair he'd placed in front of the freezer, right behind his chair. I sat there reading while Dad hummed along with the music.

A few moments later the truck jarred to a stop. I rose from my seat and looked out the driver's side window. There was a young man with short blond hair and pimply skin standing on the sidewalk, holding a small child to his chest. When Dad extended his hand, the man pulled his child away, but Dad kept his hand in the air and smiled at him. His smile was so kind, without a trace of hurt or sarcasm or shame. The man looked at Dad's extended hand and then at Dad's smile, and he slowly lifted his child toward Dad, who stroked the child's head.

The man laughed nervously. "It's sure nice to see you here. Certainly hot enough for ice cream. How much do you charge?"

Dad started, and then he turned to his right to peer at the stickers we'd affixed to the side of the truck the night before. The stickers featured artistic renderings of the ice cream bars we'd stacked in our freezer beneath islands of dry ice. As Dad stared at the stickers, I realized that we'd neglected to indicate how much each kind of ice cream would cost.

"Well, since you're our first sale, tell me what you want and how much you want to pay for it," Dad said confidently.

The man scrunched up his face and shook his head. "What did you say?"

Dad enunciated: "Choose something and pay what you want."

"How about a Creamsicle for a dollar?"

Dad motioned to me and I opened the freezer and reached into the upper left corner, where I'd carefully placed a box of Creamsicles the night before. I pulled one from the pack and handed it to Dad. Dad handed the bar to the child, who wrapped all ten little fingers around it and smiled at us in appreciation.

"Don't worry about paying. I hope to see you soon."

When they left, I grabbed the permanent marker from the desk at the front of the truck and waved it near Dad's face.

"Daddy, we need to mark the prices on the stickers!"

"No, let's wait. Let's see what happens."

My father continued to drive around the city without any plan. Sometimes we passed down the same street twice, and whenever someone called to us we'd stop and let them decide the price. Dad spoke in short, declarative sentences, and he asked me to speak if our customers had more questions. We gave some ice cream away, and we sold some for a couple dollars apiece. As darkness came on, we drove back home a few dollars richer.

Tayo, Femi, and I were already out of the truck when Dad reminded us that we had to move the boxes of ice cream from the dead freezer in the truck to the grunting freezer in the garage. We quickly emptied the freezer in the truck, and when we saw the mess inside the freezer in the garage we called Dad. He ran to us, and when he saw it he stepped back and cursed loudly.

The freezer was lukewarm and the ice on the sides had melted. A congealed multi-colored mass of melted ice cream had pooled on the bottom. The freezer had failed.

Dad stood staring at the ground and we waited because we didn't know what we were supposed to do. He turned around and began walking back to the truck.

"Help me put all the ice cream back into the truck," he called.

We did as we were told, and just as we were finishing Dad started up the engine.

"Tunde, follow me."

I bounded into the truck, and we went off to buy more dry ice.

Tayo, Femi, and I felt Dad's heat when he entered our bedroom the following morning, so we woke up before he could shout at us. We dressed quickly and ran to the truck. I opened the freezer and saw the evaporating islands of dry ice atop the boxes. I pressed the packages of ice cream with my index finger; they felt firm and cold. We were already prepared—sitting in the back of the truck, reading studiously—by the time Dad climbed into the driver's seat. He looked back at us without saying a word, and then he started the engine.

"Daddy, what about the prices?" I asked tentatively.

Dad switched off the ignition and left the truck with the permanent marker. I went out with him and he looked down at me.

"So what should we do?"

I'd been thinking about it all night and I'd prepared an answer: "Why don't we make everything fifty cents?"

Dad smiled for the first time.

"Do you know how much each ice cream cost me? And I have to pay for gas, dry ice, and make enough for us to eat."

"Okay, how about fifty-five cents?"

Dad laughed.

"Who are you trying to help? Your family? Or the strangers who will be buying from us? You must learn that there are times to be nice, and there are times to be mean." With that Dad handed me the marker, and he called out the prices as I pointed to each of the stickers. I copied down the prices in neat blocky script.

Our second day on the road was quite different from our first. Dad drove with purpose this time, and we passed by more schools and playgrounds. He didn't laugh with us as he had the day before; he kept his eyes on the side of the road, searching for anyone with even the smallest quantity of desire in their eyes. Our first sale came much more quickly. After about ten minutes on the road, we were flagged down by three teenagers on a playground.

"Hey, man! We didn't know anyone sold ice cream around here! Whaddya got?"

Dad pointed to the side of the truck. "Pick whatever you like, I have a full freezer today, gentlemen."

I peered at each of them, hoping I'd recognize a friend, or at least an acquaintance. I wanted desperately to meet someone I knew, someone who would return to school and tell everyone that my father sold ice cream. I knew it was my only chance at the kind of popularity I'd coveted my entire life. Once word got out, people would want to know more about my father, more about my family, and—most importantly—more about me. I had all my answers ready.

(I stopped caring by the middle of the summer. The few times I saw people I knew, I could tell from the way they looked at me that they still thought I was a loser. I mean, who was I trying to kid? My parents were still from Africa, I still had a weird name, and we still weren't Mormons. A little ice-cream selling wasn't going to change any of that.)

We stayed on the road past sundown, and by the time we pulled onto our street Femi was sleeping on the bed in the back, and I'd already exchanged places with Tayo at least twice. When I opened the freezer I noticed that it was half-empty, and our makeshift cash register at the front of the truck was filled with one-dollar bills. Dad rubbed his eyes after parking, and he cleared his throat the way he always did when he had an announcement.

"We did okay today, guys. We'll do better tomorrow."

Then he stepped out of the driver's seat, and we packed more dry ice into the freezer.

By the end of our first week on the road, we'd developed a system. Dad insisted that I accompany him each day while Tayo and Femi rotated during weekdays (someone had to stay home and look after Ade). Mom would rise before us each day to prepare our meals for the road, which she placed in used Styrofoam packaging that had formerly held Chinese food or hamburgers. At midday Dad would stop at a parking lot somewhere and we would swallow our cold *fufu* or *jollof* rice or fried plantain, and then we'd start out again.

We did better as it got hotter. By the middle of the summer, as word spread about our ice-cream truck, we'd drive onto certain streets and a hungry crowd would have already gathered. Tayo, Femi, or I would hustle at the freezer while the kids and adults called out their orders. Some days we woke up well before dawn to buy more ice cream from the wholesalers downtown.

*

In late July, one of our regular customers—he lived three streets down from us, quite near my elementary school—suggested that we park our truck on Main Street during the annual Middleton City Fair.

"You'll make a killing!" the man said, smiling. "There's never any ice cream around—you should jump on it before someone else gets the same idea!"

Dad asked for more information and the man told him everything—that the fair took place on the Friday and Saturday of Labor Day weekend, just before school started; how the fairgrounds extended all the way down Main Street, right through the middle of town; how there were kiosks for everything: cotton candy, caramel apples, and popcorn; how there were games and a few rides; how there were even a few people who sold snow cones from small coolers, but no ice-cream trucks.

We'd never heard of the fair, even though we'd been living in Middleton for two years, and as the man described one spectacle after another I wondered how something so wonderful had escaped our attention for so long. We were partly to blame, I knew—we mostly stayed to ourselves. We hadn't really traveled much around the city, and my parents didn't have any friends. Our house was a miniature Nigeria, with its own customs and culture, and I didn't know much about the world outside. I interpreted our ignorance of the Middleton

City Fair as just another sign that we would never truly fit in Utah, that the various mysteries of the place would forever remain closed to us, because we weren't Mormon, because we were black.

Dad suddenly became infatuated with the fair, and for the rest of the day he spoke of nothing else. He talked himself into the idea that the Middleton City Fair was the reason he'd started selling ice cream in the first place, that God's will had been revealed to him through the words of one of his favorite customers. By the time we returned home that evening the Middleton City Fair had become something we'd been waiting for all our lives. Dad went to City Hall first thing the following morning and applied for a vendor's license. He returned disappointed; he told us that they'd asked him to fill out a few forms, that they'd said they would contact him in a few days. But we didn't hear anything from them in the following weeks, despite the fact that Dad pestered them continually. He even drafted Tayo and me into the cause of calling the city council to plead our case. "These people always respond better to an American accent," he said. So he called, and we called. We even assumed bland American names and bland American accents on the phone, but we garnered no response.

Meanwhile, our ice-cream business was going so well that Dad decided to purchase another U. S. Postal Service truck. He left with Mom early one morning in August for Salt Lake City and they both returned driving trucks, Dad behind the wheel of our ice-cream truck, and Mom driving a retired mail truck. After we quickly converted the mail truck into an ice-cream truck, Dad helped us pull the dead freezer out of our first truck and into the garage, and then he drove off again. He beeped loudly when he returned, and we saw a U-Haul trailer attached to the truck. We opened the trailer to a new freezer, and as we laughed Dad said, "And this one works!" He opened the back of the truck to reveal another new freezer.

We helped Dad carry the new freezer out of the trailer and into the new truck, and then we went inside to rest. Dad came into the living room shortly afterward and asked us what we were doing. He'd already changed into his customary ice-cream-selling outfit—a loose-fitting, dark blue, short-sleeve dress shirt, and dark blue slacks. Femi and I ran outside and hopped into the new truck as Dad was starting it, and we went off for a half-day of selling.

*

Dad spent a week trying to find someone to drive the second truck. He placed an ad in the paper and finally settled on a twenty-four-year-old named Jerry, whom he liked because Jerry had referred to him as "sir." Jerry claimed he was trying to save enough money to return to college, and Dad liked that story, too. Tayo and I didn't tell Dad about the time we caught Jerry smoking in the backyard while he was waiting for Dad to return from the wholesale ice-cream warehouse with ice cream for his truck.

I don't know what kind of pay arrangement my father worked out with Jerry, but after only a week of working together Jerry simply stopped showing up. When Tayo asked Dad at dinner what had happened, he told us not to worry. "I will find someone better," he said.

Dad eventually found someone else to drive the second ice cream truck, and then someone else when that person quit, and then someone after that. They all eventually left because Dad drove them too hard, and because he demanded a quota of ice cream sold each day.

Dad began to push himself harder as well. He woke up at four in the morning every day so he could peer at the big map of Middleton he'd purchased early in the summer. Sometimes he'd wake me up as well, and I would try to keep my eyes open as he traced new paths of ice-cream dominance in red ink—scribbling red lines next to other red lines, crossing out some routes completely, like he was planning his takeover of the city. When he was done he'd leave the map on the table for one of us to fold up, and he'd walk whistling out the door, his new route inscribed in his brain.

We drove for longer hours each day, and Dad became adept at ingratiating himself with every person he met on the road. If he saw an old woman crossing the street he'd lower the music and speak coolly to her, his voice like a blast of cold air from an oscillating fan: "Madame! You look so lovely! How are you this afternoon? Can I interest you in a Creamsicle to help ease you on your way?"

And even if she rejected his advances, even if she ignored him completely, Dad would continue smiling. "Well, God bless you! And I expect you to buy something the next time I see you!"

At night, after I'd put on my pajamas and before I fell asleep, Dad would ask me to sit next to him at the kitchen table, and together we would read passages from my favorite books. I would read a few paragraphs and then Dad would repeat them, mimicking my tone, my accent, the way my lips wrapped themselves around each word. Over time, he began to sound like me.

*

August suddenly became September. We were stopped more often as we drove down the streets of Middleton, and the crowds that gathered to meet us at our high-traffic areas grew larger. But the entire time I couldn't stop thinking about the fair. I wondered if we'd be able to sell ice cream there. I wondered how our lives would change if they allowed us to participate; if, at the end, I would finally understand what it meant to be a part of a community.

We finally heard from the city council a few days before the fair, and it was good news. Dad immediately went to the ice cream wholesalers and placed his largest order of the summer.

"Business must be going well," the man said as he handed over box after box of ice cream.

"You have no idea," Dad said as he handed the boxes to me. "I might be putting you out of business soon."

They both laughed too loudly.

On the first day of the fair we all woke up at 4 A.M. and began to make preparations. Mom brewed two big pots of stew and pulled the *moin moin* she'd prepared the night before from the fridge. While she fried up some plantains, the rest of us packed each freezer as full of ice cream as we could, and Dad and Freddy—Dad had hired him the day before—left with both trucks to buy dry ice. When they returned, we stashed the food in the back of the trucks and stepped in so Dad and Freddy could drive us to Main Street. Mom and Ade followed in our Chevy.

When we arrived, we saw other vendors preparing for the day and policemen going from stand to stand, asking to see vendor passes. The policemen came to our trucks and Dad proudly showed them ours. They nodded and continued on. Dad asked us to gather in a circle and hold hands. We prayed together under the rising sun.

"God, we thank you for your blessings. We thank you that we are the first ice-cream vendors who have been allowed to participate in this festival, Oh Lord. We didn't know about this festival before now, but we thank you that we learned in time, and that we were blessed with an opportunity to be here. God, please bless us today, so that the line of people who ask us for ice cream will not stop. You have finally given us an opportunity to make it in this country. This is our chance. Help us to make the most of it."

We said a loud "Amen" together, and my father became a different person. He peeled off his smile.

He pointed at Freddy. "Go and park where I told you to park last night. Stay there. Tayo will go with you. If anything happens, send him down to this truck with a message. Do not mess around today. I am not playing with you. This is the day that can make the rest of our lives."

Freddy slinked away, scowling, and Tayo and Ade followed him. Dad turned to the rest of us.

"I chose this part of the street for a reason. According to my sources in city hall, the busiest part of the festival will be here. That means we'll be working nonstop. Mom already knows that she'll have to go back home if we need more food, or if we need more ice cream. Tunde, Femi, I need everything you have today. You cannot let up. Keep moving forward, no matter what."

We both nodded.

We sat in the truck and waited as the sun continued its upward path. The chaos around our truck began slowly. Outside, jugglers threw bright balls into the air, and loud music began pumping from large speakers. The music was so loud that I could almost see the musical notes curling up out of the speakers. A man came walking by with a card deck, and he flashed a few cards at Femi and me as we peered out of the driver's side window. Our eyes flashed in response, but we felt Dad's hard gaze knocking on our backs, so we turned away from him.

People of all kinds began to walk around, and a few of them stopped by our truck. I stood ready at the freezer and passed Dad the ice cream they were asking for before their tongues had formed the second syllable. As the day grew hotter, more people stopped by, and soon a line snaked around our truck and down the length of the street for many feet. Femi and I worked together, huffing and puffing into the freezer, developing a rhythm of delivery while Dad worked complex figures in his head and passed the ice cream to our customers. By eleven, we were on the verge of running out of a few items, and Dad sent me to the other truck to see if we could get any more supplies from them.

I saw the long line as I approached the other truck, and knocked on the back door. Tayo opened it for me, and then he rushed back to Freddy with a package of ice cream in his hand. Ade was playing with a ball on the bed, and he giggled at me when I waved. I asked Tayo if they had any extra boxes of snow cones or Fudgsicles, and he shook his head.

I sprinted back and told Dad the news, and he dispatched Mom to the house to pick up more ice cream. We were already out of a few items by the time she returned, and a great cheer rose up as she walked through the crowd, carrying boxes of ice cream above her head.

I placed my hand on my father's shoulder, and he turned and smiled at me. His smile was wide and wondrous. Suddenly I wanted to hug him and tell him it would always be like this. I wanted to tell him that he would always be a star. I wanted to live in this moment for the rest of my life, to forget what I had seen while I was out trying to get more ice cream for the truck.

Just before I reached Freddy's truck, I noticed a few men standing in a circle a few feet down the street. One of them was licking one of our Firecracker Popsicles. The Firecracker looked delicious; its red, white, and blue segments sparkled in the sun. The man pulled the Firecracker from his mouth and oinked loudly, and then he began to speak in a melodramatic, garbled manner. Spittle flew from his lips. I couldn't make out what he was saying. In the midst of his performance I heard him say "Creamsicle"; the other men laughed and slapped their thighs. That's when I realized they were making fun of my father. I ignored them and kept walking.

I already knew that the weather was growing colder, and that my brothers and I would soon be returning to school. I knew that in a few days my father would park his trucks for the winter, that the moment he did so he would just be an immigrant again. But I also knew that my father was content. I knew he was calm and proud. I knew that—for the first time in a long time—he was in control. He had achieved everything he set out to achieve.

And besides—our day was just beginning. We had more ice cream to sell. And the weather was perfect. I knew that we were going to sell more ice cream than we'd ever sold before.

Tomorrow was coming, but I was happy. My father still had a few hours left in the sun.

THANK YOU, M'AM

Langston Hughes

She was a large woman with a large purse that had every-thing in it but a hammer and nails. It had a long strap, and she carried it slung across her shoulder. It was about eleven o'clock at night, dark, and she was walking alone, when a boy ran up behind her and tried to snatch her purse. The strap broke with the sudden single tug the boy gave it from behind. But the boy's weight and the weight of the purse combined caused him to lose his balance. Instead of taking off full blast as he had hoped, the boy fell on his back on the sidewalk and his legs flew up. The large woman simply turned around and kicked him right square in his blue-jeaned sitter. Then she reached down, picked the boy up by his shirt front, and shook him until his teeth rattled.

After that the woman said, "Pick up my pocketbook, boy, and give it here."

She still held him tightly. But she bent down enough to permit him to stoop and pick up her purse. Then she said, "Now ain't you ashamed of yourself?"

Firmly gripped by his shirt front, the boy said, "Yes'm."

The woman said, "What did you want to do it for?"

The boy said, "I didn't aim to."

She said, "You a lie!"

By that time two or three people passed, stopped, turned to look, and some stood watching.

"If I turn you loose, will you run?" asked the woman.

"Yes'm," said the boy.

"Then I won't turn you loose," said the woman. She did not release him.

"Lady, I'm sorry," whispered the boy.

"Um-hum! Your face is dirty. I got a great mind to wash your face for you. Ain't you got nobody home to tell you to wash your face?"

"No'm," said the boy.

"Then it will get washed this evening," said the large woman, starting up the street, dragging the frightened boy behind her.

He looked as if he were fourteen or fifteen, frail and willow-wild, in tennis shoes and blue jeans.

The woman said, "You ought to be my son. I would teach you right from wrong. Least I can do right now is to wash your face. Are you hungry?"

"No'm," said the being-dragged boy. "I just want you to turn me loose."

"Was I bothering you when I turned that corner?" asked the woman.

"No'm."

"But you put yourself in contact with *me*," said the woman. "If you think that that contact is not going to last awhile, you got another thought coming. When I get through with you, sir, you are going to remember Mrs. Luella Bates Washington Jones."

Sweat popped out on the boy's face and he began to struggle. Mrs. Jones stopped, jerked him around in front of her, put a half nelson about his neck, and continued to drag him up the street. When she got to her door, she dragged the boy inside, down a hall, and into a large kitchenette-furnished room at the rear of the house. She switched on the light and left the door open. The boy could hear other roomers laughing and talking in the large house. Some of their doors were open, too, so he knew he and the woman were not alone. The woman still had him by the neck in the middle of her room.

She said, "What is your name?"

"Roger," answered the boy.

"Then, Roger, you go to that sink and wash your face," said the woman, whereupon she turned him loose—at last. Roger looked at the door—looked at the woman—looked at the door—*and went to the sink.*

"Let the water run until it gets warm," she said. "Here's a clean towel."

"You gonna take me to jail?" asked the boy, bending over the sink.

"Not with that face, I would not take you nowhere," said the woman. "Here I am trying to get home to cook me a bite to eat, and you snatch my pocketbook! Maybe you ain't been to your supper either, late as it be. Have you?"

"There's nobody home at my house," said the boy.

"Then we'll eat," said the woman. "I believe you're hungry—or been hungry—to try to snatch my pocketbook!"

"I want a pair of blue suede shoes," said the boy.

"Well, you didn't have to snatch *my* pocketbook to get some suede shoes," said Mrs. Luella Bates Washington Jones. "You could of asked me."

"M'am?"

The water dripping from his face, the boy looked at her. There was a long pause. A very long pause. After he had dried his face, and not knowing what else to do, dried it again, the boy turned around, wondering what next. The door was open. He could make a dash for it down the hall. He could run, run, run, *run!*

The woman was sitting on the daybed. After a while she said, "I were young once and I wanted things I could not get."

There was another long pause. The boy's mouth opened. Then he frowned, not knowing he frowned.

The woman said, "Um-hum! You thought I was going to say *but,* didn't you? You thought I was going to say, *but I didn't snatch people's pocketbooks.* Well, I wasn't going to say that." Pause. Silence. "I have done things, too, which I would not tell you, son—neither tell God, if He didn't already know. Everybody's got something in common. So you set down while I fix us something to eat. You might run that comb through your hair so you will look presentable."

In another corner of the room behind a screen was a gas plate and an icebox. Mrs. Jones got up and went behind the screen. The woman did not watch the boy to see if he was going to run now, nor did she watch her purse, which she left behind her on the daybed. But the boy took care to sit on the far side of the room, away from the purse, where he thought she could easily see him out of the corner of her eye if she wanted to. He did not trust the woman *not* to trust him. And he did not want to be mistrusted now.

"Do you need somebody to go to the store," asked the boy, "maybe to get some milk or something?"

"Don't believe I do," said the woman, "unless you just want sweet milk yourself. I was going to make cocoa out of this canned milk I got here."

"That will be fine," said the boy.

She heated some lima beans and ham she had in the icebox, made the cocoa, and set the table. The woman did not ask the boy anything about where he lived, or his folks, or anything else that would embarrass him. Instead, as they ate, she told him about her job in a hotel beauty shop that stayed open late, what the work was like, and how all kinds of women came in and out, blonds, redheads, and Spanish. Then she cut him a half of her ten-cent cake.

"Eat some more, son," she said.

When they were finished eating, she got up and said, "Now here, take this ten dollars and buy yourself some blue suede shoes. And next time, do not make the mistake of latching onto *my* pocketbook *nor nobody else's*—because shoes got by devilish ways will burn your feet. I got to get my rest now. But from here on in, son, I hope you will behave yourself."

She led him down the hall to the front door and opened it.

"Good night! Behave yourself, boy!" she said, looking out into the street as he went down the steps.

The boy wanted to say something other than, "Thank you, M'am," to Mrs. Luella Bates Washington Jones, but although his lips moved, he couldn't even say that as he turned at the foot of the barren stoop and looked up at the large woman in the door. Then she shut the door.

BUSINESS AT ELEVEN

Toshio Mori

When he came to our house one day and knocked on the door and immediately sold me a copy of *The Saturday Evening Post*, it was the beginning of our friendship and also the beginning of our business relationship.

His name is John. I call him Johnny and he is eleven. It is the age when he should be crazy about baseball or football or fishing. But he isn't. Instead he came again to our door and made a business proposition.

"I think you have many old magazines here," he said.

"Yes," I said, "I have magazines of all kinds in the basement."

"Will you let me see them?" he said.

"Sure," I said.

I took him down to the basement where the stacks of magazines stood in the corner. Immediately this little boy went over to the piles and lifted a number of magazines and examined the dates of each number and the names.

"Do you want to keep these?" he said.

"No. You can have them," I said.

"No. I don't want them for nothing," he said. "How much do you want for them?"

"You can have them for nothing," I said.

"No, I want to buy them," he said. "How much do you want for them?"

This was a boy of eleven, all seriousness and purpose.

"What are you going to do with the old magazines?"

"I am going to sell them to people," he said.

We arranged the financial matters satisfactorily. We agreed he was to pay three cents for each copy he took home. On the first day he took home an *Esquire,* a couple of old *Saturday Evening Posts,* a *Scribner's,* an *Atlantic Monthly,* and a *Collier's.* He said he would be back soon to buy more magazines.

When he came back several days later, I learned his name was John so I began calling him Johnny.

"How did you make out, Johnny?" I said.

"I sold them all," he said. "I made seventy cents altogether."

"Good for you," I said. "How do you manage to get seventy cents for old magazines?"

Johnny said as he made the rounds selling *The Saturday Evening Post,* he also asked the folks if there were any back numbers they particularly wanted. Sometimes, he said, people will pay unbelievable prices for copies they had missed and wanted very much to see some particular articles or pictures, or their favorite writers' stories.

"You are a smart boy," I said.

"Papa says, if I want to be a salesman, be a good salesman," Johnny said. "I'm going to be a good salesman."

"That's the way to talk," I said. "And what does your father do?"

"Dad doesn't do anything. He stays at home," Johnny said.

"Is he sick or something?" I said.

"No, he isn't sick," he said. "He's all right. There's nothing wrong with him."

"How long have you been selling *The Saturday Evening Post?*" I asked.

"Five years," he said. "I began at six."

"Your father is lucky to have a smart boy like you for a son," I said.

That day he took home a dozen or so of the old magazines. He said he had five standing orders, an *Esquire* issue of June 1937, *Atlantic Monthly* February 1938 number, a copy of December 11, 1937 issue of *The New Yorker, Story Magazine* of

February 1934, and a *Collier's* of April 2, 1938. The others, he said, he was taking a chance at.

"I can sell them," Johnny said.

Several days later I saw Johnny again at the door.

"Hello, Johnny," I said. "Did you sell them already?"

"Not all," he said. "I have two left. But I want some more."

"All right," I said. "You must have good business."

"Yes," he said, "I am doing pretty good these days. I broke my own record selling *The Saturday Evening Post* this week."

"How much is that?" I said.

"I sold one hundred sixty-seven copies this week," he said. "Most boys feel lucky if they sell seventy-five or one hundred copies. But not for me."

"How many are there in your family, Johnny?" I said.

"Six counting myself," he said. "There is my father, three smaller brothers, and two small sisters."

"Where's your mother?" I said.

"Mother died a year ago," Johnny said.

He stayed in the basement a good one hour sorting out the magazines he wished. I stood by and talked to him as he lifted each copy and inspected it thoroughly. When I asked him if he had made a good sale with the old magazines recently, he said yes. He sold the *Scribner's* Fiftieth Anniversary Issue for sixty cents. Then he said he made several good sales with *Esquire* and a *Vanity Fair* this week.

"You have a smart head, Johnny," I said. "You have found a new way to make money."

Johnny smiled and said nothing. Then he gathered up the fourteen copies he picked out and said he must be going now.

"Johnny," I said, "hereafter you pay two cents a copy. That will be enough."

Johnny looked at me.

"No," he said. "Three cents is all right. You must make a profit, too."

An eleven-year-old boy—I watched him go out with his short business-like stride.

Next day he was back early in the morning. "Back so soon?" I said.

"Yesterday's were all orders," he said. "I want some more today."

"You certainly have a good trade," I said.

"The people know me pretty good. And I know them pretty good," he said. And about ten minutes later he picked out seven copies and said that was all he was taking today.

"I am taking Dad shopping," he said. "I am going to buy a new hat and shoes for him today."

"He must be tickled," I said.

"You bet he is," Johnny said. "He told me to be sure and come home early."

So he said he was taking these seven copies to the customers who ordered them and then running home to get Dad.

Two days later Johnny wanted some more magazines. He said a Mr. Whitman, who lived up a block, wanted all the magazines with Theodore Dreiser's stories inside. Then he went on talking about other customers of his. Miss White, the schoolteacher, read Hemingway, and he said she would buy back copies with Hemingway stories anytime he brought them in. Some liked Sinclair Lewis, others Saroyan, Faulkner, Steinbeck, Mann, Faith Baldwin, Fannie Hurst, Thomas Wolfe. So it went. It was amazing how an eleven-year-old boy could remember the customers' preferences and not get mixed up.

One day I asked him what he wanted to do when he grew up. He said he wanted a book shop all his own. He said he would handle old books and old magazines as well as the new ones and own the biggest bookstore around the Bay Region.

"That is a good ambition," I said. "You can do it. Just keep up the good work and hold your customers."

On the same day, in the afternoon, he came around to the house holding several packages.

"This is for you," he said, handing over a package.

"What is this?" I said.

Johnny laughed. "Open up and see for yourself," he said.

I opened it. It was a book rest, a simple affair but handy.

"I am giving these to all my customers," Johnny said.

"This is too expensive to give away, Johnny," I said. "You will lose all your profits."

"I picked them up cheap," he said. "I'm giving these away so the customers will remember me."

"That is right, too," I said. "You have good sense."

After that he came in about half a dozen times, each time taking with him ten or twelve copies of various magazines. He said he was doing swell. Also, he said he was now selling *Liberty* along with the *Saturday Evening Posts.*

Then for two straight weeks I did not see him once. I could not understand this. He had never missed coming to the house in two or three days. Something must be wrong, I thought. He must be sick, I thought.

One day I saw Johnny at the door. "Hello, Johnny," I said. "Where were you? Were you sick?"

"No. I wasn't sick," Johnny said.

"What's the matter? What happened?" I said.

"I'm moving away," Johnny said. "My father is moving to Los Angeles."

"Sit down, Johnny," I said. "Tell me all about it."

He sat down. He told me what had happened in two weeks. He said his dad went and got married to a woman he, Johnny, did not know. And now, his dad and this woman say they are moving to Los Angeles. And about all there was for him to do was to go along with them.

"I don't know what to say, Johnny," I said.

Johnny said nothing. We sat quietly and watched the time move.

"Too bad you will lose your good trade," I finally said.

"Yes. I know," he said. "But I can sell magazines in Los Angeles."

"Yes, that is true," I said.

Then he said he must be going. I wished him good luck. We shook hands. "I will come and see you again," he said.

"And when I visit Los Angeles some day," I said, "I will see you in the largest bookstore in the city."

Johnny smiled. As he walked away, up the street and out of sight, I saw the last of him walking like a good businessman, walking briskly, energetically, purposefully.

HALLOWEEN

Norma Elia Cantú

It's Halloween, but we haven't donned costumes—we didn't yet believe in that strange U.S. custom: only my younger siblings did many years later. Mamagrande and her oldest daughter, Tía Lydia, have come to visit, to clean the lápida in Nuevo Laredo where Mamagrande's dead children are buried, to place fresh flowers in tin cans wrapped in foil and hang beautiful wreaths; they've come to honor the dead. But it's the day before, and Mami and Papi and Bueli leave me alone with our guests and the kids; I'm fixing dinner—showing off that I can cook and feed the kids. I've made flour tortillas, measuring ingredients with my hands, the way Mami and Bueli do, five handfuls of flour, some salt, a handful of shortening, some espauda from the red can marked "KC." Once it's all mixed in, the shortening broken into bits no bigger than peas, I pour hot water, almost boiling but not quite, and knead the dough, shape it into a fat ball like a bowl turned over. I let it set while I prepare the sauce I will use for the fideo. When it's time, I form the small testales the size of my small fist; I roll out the tortillas, small and round, the size of saucers, and cook them on the comal. As they cook, I pile them up on a dinner plate, wrap them in a cloth embroidered with a garland of tiny flowers—red, blue, yellow—and crochet-edged in pale pink. We eat fideo, beans, tortillas quietly because Mamagrande and Tía Lydia watch us. We drink the cinnamon tea with milk. I look outside and see a huge moon rising; it's the same color as the warm liquid in my cup. Later, Tino and Dahlia wash the dishes, and even later, the kids are watching TV quietly, without arguing. Mamagrande rocks in the sillón out on the porch and can't understand why some kids all ragged and costumed as hoboes and clowns come and ask for treats. I try to explain, but it's useless. My siblings want "fritos" so I cut some corn tortillas Mamagrande has brought from Monterrey into strips and heat the grease in an old skillet. I'm busily frying the strips and soaking the grease off on a clean dishrag when all of a sudden the skillet turns, and I see the hot grease fall as if in slow motion. My reflexes are good, but the burning on my foot tells me I wasn't fast enough. At first it doesn't hurt, but then I feel it, the skin and to the bone, as if a million cactus thorns—the tiny nopal thorns—have penetrated my foot. I scream with pain. Mamagrande rushes and puts butter on the burn. I cry. The kids are scared. Later, Doña Lupe will have to do healings de susto—they're so frightened. And when Mami and Papi return, they scold me for not being careful.

I miss school for two days. When I go back, my foot and ankle wrapped in gauze and cotton bandages attract attention. I'm embarrassed. When my social studies teacher, Mrs. Kazen, the wife of a future senator, concerned, asks, I tell her the truth.

"Did you go to the hospital? Did a doctor examine the burn?"

"No," I say, knowing it's the wrong answer, but not wanting to lie.

She shakes her head, so I know not to tell her how every three hours, day and night for three days, Mami, remembering Bueli's remedios, has been putting herb poultices on the burn and cleaning it thoroughly. She's punctured the water-filled ámpula with a maguey thorn and tells me there won't even be a scar. And there isn't.

LA CIRAMELLA

Mary K. Mazotti

"**N**othing in the house to do?" I heard Papa say as I sat reading on the steps of the front porch. He towered before
me like a yellow giant. Papa had just finished sulfuring our
vineyard across the dirt road and was covered with the yellow
powder.

"We did everything you told us, Papa," I answered, speaking
for my two younger sisters and myself. He grunted with satisfaction. Idle daughters always set him on edge, as busyness was
Papa's way of life. He turned and walked slowly to the faucet
trough to wash up for our main meal of the day. I carefully
pinched a rose leaf from the trellis to make a bookmark and
scooted inside to set the table. It was a spring Saturday, 1936,
and six long years into the Depression.

Each early spring the sun's bright rising was directly over
our vineyard and small house. In spite of the Depression,
Mama saw the wand of golden rays as a blessing for her and
Papa, and their three young daughters born in America. Times
in America could never match the poverty of their native rocky
villages in southern Italy. And Mama never stopped pouring
out words of gratitude for finding a better life.

Papa was famished from spraying sulfur all morning. Now he
seemed content that the new grapes were protected from mil-
dew. He sniffed the homemade noodles Mama had prepared.

"*Una festa!*" he spoke through his nostrils. Mama had tossed
the noodles with hot olive oil, minced garlic, and fresh basil,
and sprinkled over them her grated goat cheese.

"*Pronto,*" Mama said, putting the steaming platter carefully on the round oak table. Making a swift blessing over our food, Mama served everyone.

I watched Mama's flushed cheeks as she ate. I knew she was hungry. Early that morning she had heated tubs of water on a fire pit outside to wash clothes. She stood stooped for hours scrubbing bed sheets and towels on the scrub board, twisting and twisting out suds and rinse water, and then pinning them to wire lines strung on the sunny side of the house, where carnations and hollyhocks bloomed. Needless to say, I and my sisters, Lomena and Pina, felt hunger rumbles also from doing housework and picking up around the big yard like Papa told us to do.

Papa finished the first dish of noodles and was into his second when he got off on a conversation about how life used to be in his native village of Grisolia, where he was born. (Papa and Mama often spoke of their little villages. Mama spoke of San Sosti.) I tried hard to picture it all and liked to share these stories with my sixth-grade teacher, whom I adored and respected. Papa became very nostalgic as he recalled the fun things that happened as he grew up in Grisolia.

"The thing I itch to do most," he said, "is to play *ciramella* again." My sisters and I stared blankly.

Mama explained, "It's a music instrument—a bagpipe, made of goatskin."

Lomena and Pina giggled. Staring at my father's unshaven face, I scowled. "Goatskin!" What a stinky instrument, I was about to blurt out, but I knew better than to make fun of my father.

Papa rushed on, his face rosy, "I tell you, no one could play the goatskin like me." Laying down his fork rolled fat with noodles, he pretended playing one. With both hands uplifted, he made droning bagpipe sounds come from his nose by wrinkling it upward and humming through his teeth.

This time I laughed till the tears came. "I didn't know you were a musician, Papa," I said with amazement.

"By the saints!" he answered. "I think I'll just make one for old-time sake. It will take the place of the one I left behind in Grisolia. What a pity I was talked out of bringing it to America by *cara* Mama. I let her load me up with dried sausage and her bread instead."

My mother stopped eating. She pushed a loose hairpin into her hair bun. "*Ma*, Nichole," she teased, "what do you know about bagpipe-making?" Flinging her right hand upward, she went on, "When was the last time you've seen one?"

Papa stuck out his chin and huffed, "Elena, I can remember a sack of things! What is needed? What is needed?" he repeated, and answered for himself, "Just the skin of a young goat and pipes for playing. That's all!"

"*Sì, Sì,*" Mama argued back, with twinkling eyes and still teasing. "What little I remember the skin has to be peeled off carefully—like a sock, not slit down the middle—to make an airtight bag. And curing the skin! It's not something simple, like swatting flies."

Papa couldn't help but laugh. He liked Mama's sharp sense of humor. He then got up to take some food scraps to Primo, his dog, without saying more about the matter. I wondered, as my sister Lomena and I washed the dishes in a pan of hot water, if Papa would really make a *ciramella*.

My mother and father had met and wed in their new country of America, in the early 1920s, when thousands of Italians left families behind and sailed across oceans to find better lives in new lands. They settled in California, in the San Joaquin Valley, where young vineyards, orchards, and farmlands and small shops were already started by friends before them, and by Armenians, Greeks, Mexicans, and French.

Now, in 1936, America was still having bad times called a Depression. People were out of work. Banks were failing and families lost home and hard-worked lands because they couldn't make payments. Worse, crops were not paying much.

Papa and Mama already knew how to make do with little.

Fortunately, Papa had his land free of debt before he married Mama. And Nonna, Mama's mother, let them live in the small two-bedroom house rent-free when she moved to San Francisco. There were plenty of fruit trees and vegetables Papa had planted across the road; eggs from hens, milk from the goat, and catches of rabbits and quails by Papa. Sacks of flour and gallons of cooking oil were bought with side-job money Papa made on other ranches. And Papa was never without a bottle of homemade wine from his own vineyard to help his digestion, and to help him relax from long hours of work.

One evening the whole family walked to the east side of Clovis to visit Papa's *paesano*, Carlo, and family. Carlo and his wife, Amelia, were godparents to Lomena and me. They had a family of twelve children. I liked to visit them because their oldest daughter, Theresa, and I were good friends. We liked to giggle and talk about friends and growing up.

I had forgotten all about Papa making the bagpipe until I overheard him bring up old times in Italy to my godfather. Papa didn't say he was going to make a bagpipe; he just asked clever questions about how to make one. I thought, How wise Papa is. He still dreamed of making one, but wanted to save embarrassment if it didn't turn out right. After our visit, my godfather took us home in his old Studebaker.

As he did every springtime, Papa bought a young goat from a farmer. Besides giving the family rest from eating jackrabbits and chicken meat, the goat provided the skin for the *ciramella*. I was glad that we were in school when Papa did the butchering and skinning behind the chicken shed. Only Primo, the dog, watched. Papa got the dog from a friend and named him after Primo Carnera, an Italian world heavyweight champion boxer a few years back.

Papa had removed the skin as he wanted it—whole, except with openings at top and bottom, and where the legs stood. Then followed many weeks of scraping off the hair, and rubbing and soaking the skin to make it soft.

One day Mama complained to Papa, "*Mamma mia!* What strange things I'm putting up with these days, Nichole. You have used my washtubs to treat your *ciramella* skin and my clothes are drying an ugly smell."

"I didn't know," said Papa. "*Basta.* That's it. I'm finished with the treatments. I'll scour the tubs with wood ashes for you— that is, if you write a letter for me."

Mama pulled her black-and-white-checkered apron above her plump middle and said, "Let me guess. You want me to write to your father in Italy for the blowpipe and sounding pipes for the *ciramella.*"

"Please," said Papa, "you know how poor my writing is." So Mama did. I was proud that she had learned to write in Italian before she came to America. She even went to school in America up to the fourth grade. Papa was still struggling with his writing, and I was amazed at how fancy he could write when he made up his mind.

Every night my father pinned the bagpipe skin to the clothesline to air out. Not long after, he was heard yelling, "What happened to it? What's happened to it?" We all dashed outside. Papa was red with anger. The line was broken and the skin gone. Everyone searched at least three times, every spot of the yard. Just when the skin seemed forever lost, Papa looked in Primo's doghouse. There it was next to him. Papa shook his fist and cursed. Primo ran and hid behind the woodpile. But I knew it wasn't Primo's fault the clothesline broke.

Late October when grape leaves had turned yellow, and some purple red, and the grapes were picked, Papa brought home a package from the post office. "They have arrived," he said happily tearing open the package. Lomena and I jumped up from doing our homework and Pina from her scribbling.

"Can we watch, Papa?" Pina said, jumping up and down.

"Sure, Little Squash," answered Papa as he unwrapped the brown pipes. "And after we eat, I'll fit them into the skin."

That afternoon I carried in cut grape stumps to warm up the kitchen. The stumps threw off good heat to warm up the neat tiny living room, two bedrooms, and large kitchen eating area. Papa worked on a bench that we kept for company. As Mama toasted fava beans for munching, he marked the skin leg opening that would be used to fit in the blowpipe and valve. He fitted the sounding pipes in the neck opening and bound them in place tightly with twisted hemp. Papa neatly sewed up the bottom and remaining leg openings.

"It looks like a giant flat pear with horns," I whispered softly in Lomena's ear. She bent over with laughter.

"What's next, Papa?" said Pina, pulling on the elastic of the flannel pajamas Mama had made her.

"Air," said Papa. "Lots of it." He blew and blew into the bagpipe and rested. Then he blew until the bag got fat. He put his fingers on some piping holes and let air gush out of the others. Wails and squeaks filled the kitchen. I ran to the bedroom to hide my laughter. Lomena followed.

"What terrible music," she gasped, laughing and holding her side.

"Shhh, not so loud," I warned. "Papa will think we are disrespectful."

Before supper, each day, Papa went down to the cellar, pulled on the overhead light string, pulled down the double doors, and practiced on his *ciramella*. He played the old tunes of the old country until they came out like he wanted them to. Within days *paesanos* and friends knew there was a *ciramella* in the Bono household.

"Yes, yes," Papa admitted, "I have made a *ciramella*."

"Well, play for us," they begged.

"At Christmastime," Papa promised. So he kept them waiting until then.

School was out for Christmas vacation. My sisters and I took turns wheeling chopped wood to the kitchen door for Mama's baking. First she made the wine and honey cookies and fig bars drizzled with white frosting; then came the pretzel-shaped bread sticks with anise seeds; finally, the fried dough puffs stuffed with preserved sardines and dried red peppers that had been soaked in boiling water. Mama hummed and sang Christmas songs along with the old Philco radio in the living room.

Lomena and I made fringed napkins from the bleached flour sacks as gifts for Mama. Lomena drew sweet little violets on a corner of each napkin and we embroidered six napkins each.

The time was right for Papa. He visited friends and personally invited them for a night of *ciramella* music and Christmas joy. We decorated the living room ceiling with chains of red and green construction paper. A small red candle was lit and placed by the picture of the Christ Child upon Mama's treadle sewing machine. The bare floors had been mopped clean earlier in the day by Mama.

That evening lights shone in every room of our house. They glowed a long ways down the road. Friends with their children walked or drove up in their secondhand cars. The December air stung noses and ears as bright stars speckled the valley heavens. Our walls shook with laughter and chattering.

"Nichole, come on now! How much longer do we have to wait to hear your *ciramella?*" hollered Rocco, who had left the old country with Papa.

"Sì, Nichole, let's see this secret project you kept from us for so long," begged Pietro, the bachelor.

Papa brought in the *ciramella* from the screened-in porch. He held it high over his head for all to see.

"It's just like the ones in the old country," marveled my god-mother, Amelia.

"Sì, sì," they all agreed. "Exactly!"

The men enjoyed sipping Papa's best wine and took turns blowing air into the bagpipe, laughing all the while as it grew fatter and fatter.

Then Papa took his *ciramella*. As he blew through the bag-pipe, his fingers moved over the piping holes. Gentle wailing sounds became folk melodies of a long-ago homeland. Men and women sang songs they learned before they ever dreamed of seeing America. Tears slid down their cheeks and it became hard for them to sing.

Suddenly Papa stopped playing. "*Basta!* Enough crying!" he shouted. "We are not at a funeral parlor. We are in America! Time to be glad. Time to dance!" He began playing one tarantella after another. Women spread wide their skirts and danced around their husbands—back and forth, hands on hips, round and round each other they danced. Children found partners and did the same in corners, copying.

"*Bravo, Niccolò! Bravo!*" friends yelled.

That night Papa appeared to me as one gigantic happy glow. I wanted the night never to end.

Winter passed and then spring. As summer moved into July, a heat wave hit the valley. A terrible odor began to hang in the house.

Lomena complained loudly, "Mama, my stomach wants to throw up from the smell."

Papa sniffed his way to a shelf in the screened-in porch. "*Dio!*" he groaned. "Can it be—no, it can't be!"

"I think your bagpipe is beginning to rot inside," said Mama, holding her nose.

"What a waste," said Papa. "We could have had more fun with it."

We felt sad for Papa. Who could ever forget that Christmas night? Without another word, Papa ripped out the pipes from the *ciramella* and took the skin to the backyard. He grabbed the shovel standing upright in the dirt by the water faucet and dug a deep hole. He plopped in the skin and filled up the hole, stomping on the dirt with his shoes to seal in the odor. I watched as Papa put the shovel back where it stood before; without looking up, he strode across the road and into the vineyard.

AMERICAN DAD, 1969

Marina Budhos

There was a time when I believed my father to be the only man in Queens, New York, who could not properly hold a garden hose. He failed me in other ways too—with garden spades, lawnmowers, and barbecues—all industrious fatherly talents that flourished up and down the courtyards of Windsor Parks, the garden apartment community we lived in.

I'll say this for my father: he was a terrific toilet scrubber. He had seized on this chore when my mother began to get disgusted with a husband who only had the energy to teach high school and come home to nap and eat, and complained that he didn't do enough in the house. We don't do that back down there! he growled back at her—down there being the Caribbean. But come Sunday morning now, my father disappeared into the bathroom and from behind the door came great, slopping noises. When he finally emerged two hours later, the toilet was polished to gem-like brilliance.

The problem was, toilets were private and all I cared about at the age of eleven were public things—like soaping the car or attending PTA meetings—acts my father seemed to willfully deprive me of, all because of something called his "foreignness." I honestly didn't know what this foreignness was. It was like an aura of words and perception, invisible to me. Maybe if I could see it, I'd be a less disagreeable daughter. I'd escape those bitter freefalls of disappointment each time he failed me, like when he didn't know a slang word or could not cut my birthday cake into beautiful slices, for all my friends to see.

The spring of fifth grade, having won the spelling bee and having received an A-plus for English, I was especially furious about my father's refusal to use the word "mail." It was my job to fetch our mail from the slot and bring it to him in his bedroom, where he sorted out bills. Without fail, he always called out to me, "Come, Jamila, come! Bring me those mails!"

"Mail!" I corrected, walking up the carpeted stairs. "Say *mail!* No *s!*"

My father would peer from behind his thick glasses in confusion. "All right then," he shrugged. "Mail."

Which only infuriated me more. Why couldn't my father get mad! What a terrible burden to be the child of a foreigner whose grammar needed to be corrected.

My shame over my father was aggravated even more by my best friend, Elizabeth Heller. Elizabeth was blessed with a father who did everything my father could not; he sat on the community board, marched for civil rights, held peace parties for the Vietnam War, and dressed up as Santa for our Windsor Parks Christmas party, even though the Hellers were Jewish.

And so it was to Sol we went when things got bad at school over the war.

What happened was this: the week before, the sixth-grade girls staged a protest. They marched into Thursday assembly, black bands around their arms, and refused to sing "The Star Spangled Banner." Our teacher, Mrs. Amster—nicknamed the Hamster—who led our assemblies, was so furious, the minute she brought us back to our class she unfurled the map of the world, letting it snap against the blackboard. In a quivering voice, she whispered, "Now I'm going to tell you why we have to fight this important war." She grabbed a pointer and showed us North Vietnam. "It starts here." The pointer began to twitch, inching down the brown horn of Indochina, into the blue, open space of the Pacific. "And if we don't stop communism, you know where it will spread next?"

The entire class, wide-eyed with fright, chorused, "No, where?"

"I'll tell you where!" With a flourish of her arm, she slammed the pointer into the map. "There!"

We all stared, aghast, at where the pointer rested: Australia! New Zealand!

Even I was a little terrified, though the next Thursday assembly, Elizabeth and I joined the sixth-graders and refused to sing "The Star Spangled Banner." The Hamster blushed, fixed her gaze on us, and scolded, "If you dare act like those older brats back there, I'll make sure this is put on your permanent record!"

I giggled; Elizabeth turned pale. In fact, I'd only gone along with the protest because I hated Thursday assemblies: the required white shirts and blue or red skirts; the high-ceilinged, chilly auditorium where we stared at the Hamster's upper arms jiggling in the air as she led us in dreary, patriotic songs. Most of all, Elizabeth and I wanted to be like the sixth-grade crowd, the cool girls with straight hair that brushed the soft, bleached bottoms of their Levis; the girls who made something as noisy and unpleasant as standing up against the war seem so natural, like tossing back a cool drink.

Saturday afternoon, when we told Sol about the Hamster and "The Star Spangled Banner," he was sitting at their patio table, gluing together one of his sculptures. I always found Sol's sculptures incredibly ugly, like the rest of the Hellers' apartment, which was supposed to be very modern and American, something right out of *Life* magazine. To me, each piece of furniture looked lonely and gawky in the big, empty rooms.

"You're absolutely within your rights about not singing, girls," Sol told us. "It's a First Amendment issue. Under the letter of the law, strictly speaking, no one can prevent your freedom of expression."

"So Mrs. Amster can't make us sing?" Elizabeth asked.

"You betcha, girls." He winked and wiped his hands on a rag. "Sounds like your teacher needs a little lesson in constitutional rights."

My face began to tingle and I felt a renewed sense of outrage quicken through my veins. With my own parents the message was always much more narrow and self-serving: Go to school, don't make trouble, don't stick out, and don't open that smarty-talk mouth of yours. I savored the delicious prospect of another fight with the Hamster, bolstered by terrifically reasoned Sol Heller by my side.

"I'll tell you what, kids. If Mrs. Amster gives you a hard time, I'll represent you to the principal myself. How's that sound?" He stood, bits of wood flaking off his sweatshirt.

"Oh Dad!" Elizabeth threw her arms around her father and buried her face in his stomach.

"And what about a little Carvel for you protesters, hmm?"

I stood there, not sure whether to accept. My mother, with her stream of ready bitterness, always told me Sol Heller was a phony; he didn't know the first thing about what real people struggled with. But I too wanted to throw my arms around Sol's stomach and weep for the sense of belonging and outrage he confirmed in me.

A few evenings later, Mrs. Heller called up our house and asked if Elizabeth could stay for dinner since she and Sol were delayed at a fundraiser and then had to stop off for late-night cocktails before heading back to Windsor Parks. My mother, who'd just come home from her new secretarial job, held the receiver with one hand and sent her high heel spinning through the dining room. A skinny run showed up the length of her calf. "Of course," she drawled. "I know what a busy life you lead, Marge."

Dinner was pretty bad. My mother was furious because my father forgot to take out the pork chops for defrosting. We jabbed at our tough, wrinkled meat, not able to say much. Elizabeth stayed very polite. Elizabeth was always polite, never raising her voice, never saying a bad thing about my family, though my mother was always making nasty remarks about hers—"I'm surprised your mother only buys you those plain white pants," she'd said to her tonight. "You need something a little brighter." Elizabeth's quietness seemed a part of that discreet sense of belonging, of right and wrong that had always eluded me.

After a while, my mother lifted her tired face and glared at my father. "My God, Reginald. Look at you, shoving your food in your mouth like that! Can't you eat like a civilized human being? This is America! We eat with a fork and knife here!"

"What's the matter with you?" my father grumbled. He mashed his napkin into a crumpled ball, as he always did, rice kernels clinging to his greasy fingers.

I kept my gaze on Elizabeth. Her face was lowered and she grasped the sides of her plate, as if holding on for balance.

'This is horrible," my mother went on. "I work so hard and then I couldn't even get a bus. I don't go to any parties. I don't go anywhere. I come home and have to watch you eat." The back of her chair slammed up against the server, silverware rattling inside. "I can't stand it."

My father made an annoyed grunt. "So don't stand it." As if to spite my mother, he shoved an outrageously large forkful of rice and meat into his mouth. A trickle of kernels dribbled down his chin.

For a second, I watched the hard angles of my mother's elbows fly sideways. I wondered if this was going to be one of those awful moments in our house when she seemed to break into a thousand pieces and the room grew dark. I shut my eyes, filling myself with numbness.

But no, her voice had dipped down into reasonable tones. She was normal again. We were a normal family. "Jamila, you clear the table," she told me. "I've got better things to do." Then she left the room.

After the three of us cleared the table and loaded the dishwasher in silence, we sat out on the porch. It was an early spring night, but already the sky took on that dirty-pink summer tinge. Beyond the trees, the cars parked in the parallel slots sighed and ticked with heat long after their owners had walked away. It was that time of year when people hosed down their small gardens and brought out folding chairs in the Windsor Parks courtyards and wore last year's cotton outfits, their faces hopeful, though a light wind brushed goosebumps on their arms. It was as if everyone was doing a stage rehearsal for identical activities in the summer, when the women's hair would frizz, and we could hear the tinkle of ice cubes across the oval of grass, like small, musical chimes. It seemed so clear, so simple, and ordinary, yet it was this very ordinariness that seemed just out of reach for my family.

"Your mother's off in a bad mood again," my father commented after a while.

"Yup." I began kicking at Elizabeth's chair legs.

"I don't know, Jamila. I can never get it right. What I gone and done wrong now?"

I did not answer at first. A part of me was thrilled that he'd consulted me. Another part was mortified that he'd asked in front of Elizabeth.

"You could do more in the house," I tried.

"How can that be?" he cried. "A man earns his dollar. A man wasn't raised to fuss in a kitchen."

I cast a look at Elizabeth, who kept pulling her sweater over her hands.

"You could go to Parents Night," I suggested.

My father fell silent. I'd picked an old sore between my parents. How many times did my mother complain that my father, a math teacher for Godssakes, never once helped out with my homework. He didn't even know who his own daughter's teachers were. It was as if, in front of our frightened faces, shimmered a terrifying headline: SECOND-GENERATION DAUGHTER OF WEST INDIAN IMMIGRANT CANNOT DO LONG DIVISION. WINDS UP AS CHECK-OUT CASHIER AT WALDBAUM'S.

I was about to reach over and pat my father on the knee,

reassure him that it was okay, he didn't have to show up at Parents Night since it would probably embarrass us both, when my mother called from the window.

"Reginald, have the Hellers come home yet? It's getting very late. Did they even leave a phone number?"

She stood by the parted curtain in an aquamarine terry cloth robe, wearing a clay mask that showed the deep clefts of her cheek, her downturned mouth, like an exaggerated melancholy clown face.

"I don't know," my father mumbled.

"They could call at least."

My father said nothing.

"Tell them when they arrive that we have things to do, too." But she didn't move from the window.

"Reginald?"

My father never answered. We all stared into the night. Elizabeth, too. After a while, two headlight wands swung across the trees as a low, blue car pulled to a stop. Classical music bubbled into the air; a door opened, a disk of light crowning the bald head of Sol Heller. "So how's our two leaders?" He called out through the dark.

Marge Heller came stumbling out of her side of the car; as she wove toward us, I noticed she wore a skirt made of silvery material; a pair of silver high heels dangling from one hand. She looked to me like a woman astronaut arrived on a new planet, not anyone I would ever know. Now, she wobbled to a stop, grass bent around her ankles. From the window, my mother raised a hand—half hello, half an angry salute, her face a strange, sullen stone color. "Oh, hello," Marge giggled. "Why is everyone so gloomy?"

After that evening, I vowed to initiate my father into the finer points of being an American Dad. First off, there was his wardrobe. My father hated suits, ties, and shoes. When he came home from work, he skimmed off his shirt, his socks and shoes, then paraded around the house in a pair of flimsy boxer shorts. Sometimes he didn't even pull down the blinds.

I began to bug him. Each time he came from school, I'd already laid out a pair of newly pressed slacks, a polo shirt and dry-cleaned cardigan. "Put them on," I told him, in my most adult voice.

"But I don't like this sorta thing!" he protested.

I waggled a pair of loafers I had specially polished. "And these are for around the house."

He put the outfit on, though he told me the loafers pinched his toe corns and the cardigans made him sweat. He trudged miserably around the house, fumbling for his pen or wallet.

There still remained his hair: great, loopy curls greased with Brylcream, pompadour, fifties calypso style. I threw out the tubes. I threw out a lot of other things as well. I swept his bureau top clean of all the pennies he had collected, along with the crushed, greasy wrappers from the Jamaican meat patties he would buy after school. My afternoons were spent neatly arranging his math books and student exams, hopelessly scattered around the living room. And I corrected his grammar: to the word "mails" were now added "shrimps" and "torch" (for flashlight), "gone" instead of "went," "dere" instead of "there."

My father began to fray with irritation. His brow would fork into angry lines as he asked, "Why you have to be so high-strung, Jamila? You turning crazy like the rest of this country!"

Then I began to turn it on myself. I had always struggled to keep my bedroom in any real order. The room succumbed to an almost tidal madness: dresses and blouses twisted into one another, pennies rolled, crayons broke, socks became mysteriously unmatched. I began to rage at my own disorderliness, all of which seemed the fault of some other way of living I didn't want to know.

Something new was starting to come over me: an awareness that the world was actually split into several orders. There were the neighbors in the courtyard, who worked hard in the city all day and took the IND subway and Union Turnpike bus home, arriving wilted in their suits and polyester dresses to catch the last fragrance from the oak trees, a faint smell of exhaust lingering in the air. They cared about getting a good deal on linens during the January white sale, keeping the tough boys from nearby neighborhoods away from their cars and daughters. Above lay the Hellers, a sea layer touched with an almost godly phosphorescence, where people rode in a moonlight of parties and important meetings; where gestures mattered and words rang smooth and clear. And far below, in the muddy bottoms, swam my father, who ate with his hands and didn't give a hoot about what other people thought or whether his boxer shorts showed a tear. I found myself giddy, sick with swimming between them all.

I began to turn mischievous, full of darker, random rebellions. In my notebooks, I scribbled odd cartoons of the Hamster's flabby arms. At Thursday assembly, I flipped up the pleated bottoms of other girls' skirts to show their underwear, made them shriek with surprise. Elizabeth would watch me, chewing a hangnail. I knew she was afraid of me, and whenever I sensed she might disappear into that quiet region of politeness, I grabbed her by the wrist and dug my fingernails in until the blood showed and she let out a quiet, painful cry.

At Parents Night my father wore his best tweed jacket with suede elbow patches. Even though he should have been comfortable in school corridors, he was sweating heavily, feet clomping as he stumbled into my classroom like a prisoner released into a courtyard of other convicts.

"You must be Jamila's father!" The Hamster sat perched on the corner of her desk. Today she wore a magenta tweed suit, a sprig of plastic berries pinned to her collar. A tiny, brass, painted American flag was fastened near the buttonhole of the other collar.

"Hello, hello!" my father bellowed, heading for the chair she offered. Then he halted. He wasn't sure what to do first: sit down or shake her hand. Instead he started to bellow again while he stood about a foot away. "What do you think of my daughter as a student? She doing all right? She a good girl?"

Since the Hamster didn't respond at first, he decided to shake hands and sit at the same time, yanking her arm as he dropped with a grunt into his chair, raincoat bulging on his lap. A quiet, anxious trickle began leaking down my spine.

The Hamster's hands were folded in her lap; one plump calf swung back and forth. On her face spread that familiar sickening smile I hated. "As you are probably aware, Jamila is a very bright girl. Very bright. On the Iowa Standardized Reading Tests she scored a nine-plus, which means she reads well above her own grade level. And she's doing good in math. She masters the new math concepts with great ease."

A more dazzling show of relief could not have bloomed on the face of a father who's just learned his terminally sick kid was cured. Thick streams of sweat trickled from his hair roots. "I'm so glad!" he mumbled and jumped from his chair.

The Hamster held up a palm, plastic berries jiggling. "But there's another issue I wish to discuss with you, Mr. Lukhoo." The Hamster's eyes took on a misty, sentimental gleam. I never knew exactly the meaning behind this expression, but I understood it was calculated to make me feel guilty.

"Mr. Lukhoo," she went on, "if you don't mind my asking, are you an American citizen?"

My father made a motion to straighten in his chair, but he was too big for the narrow seat. His lower lip pulled tight against his teeth. "I'm a teacher. I'm a math teacher, like you. Almost ten years now. Board of Education, Andrew Jackson High—"

"Then you especially understand our duty as educators to convey a sense of citizenship and responsibility to our students."

I knew my father had heard only one word: citizenship. I had a sudden urge to reach a hand out and cover his frightened eyes with my palm. Instead I watched in silence as he began to squirm and shuffle his feet. The tips of his curly black hair were wet. "What you getting at?"

"I'm talking about Jamila's refusal to sing 'The Star Spangled Banner.'"

"She what?" His gaze swung to me.

"It's really quite terrible," she went on. "To think of our poor young men risking their *lives* overseas. Saving *us*. And your daughter and a few others, who will go unmentioned, acting with such *disrespect*. It's a shame, Mr. Lukhoo. A terrible shame."

My hands were jammed into a tight, sweaty ball in my skirt. I couldn't look at my father.

"What's the matter with you, Jamila?" my father cried. "Why you not listen to your teacher?"

"Because."

"But you can't be going about with ideas of your own!"

I didn't answer. I imagined myself sitting at the Heller's patio table, calmly collecting Sol's clean and righteous words. The sensation was very pleasant, as if my mind was a slender bottle, filling up with lovely bright pebbles.

"The thing about Jamila is she's very intelligent, very quick," Mrs. Amster remarked. "But sometimes she turns a bit aggressive. She gets these ideas in her head. They're often, well, not very reasoned, if you get my drift."

My father sat in a crushed heap in his seat. He could not even look at me.

I don't know what happened next but I remember jumping up and waving my arms in the air. Sounds clattered out of my throat, harsh with anger. "Elizabeth's father says I have a right!" I shrieked. "Sol Heller says it's in the Constitution! I can go to the principal!"

"See what I mean?"

The two of them stared at me. The laughter of parents shot like fireworks behind the door.

Then I burst into tears. My speech seemed as stupid as my father's. He opened and shut his mouth, as if he could not breathe. Shame came pouring through me, black and dirty, burying those beautiful words of a moment before. I was ashamed for everything and at myself for having embarrassed my father. And then I was ashamed all over again for doing the very thing I'd always faulted my father for. I'd let strangers see inside.

On the drive back, my father kept getting lost, so we looped round and round the Grand Central Parkway. "See what you done!" he complained. "You got me so upset, I can't even drive proper!"

I said nothing. Why was it that whenever my father was upset with me, his anger became hopelessly mixed up with his own confusion in this country? Another terrible headline seemed to flash across the windshield: WEST INDIAN FATHER DRIVES CAR THROUGH HIGHWAY BARRIER. SAYS HE WAS IN DESPAIR OVER PARENTS NIGHT.

As we were getting out of the car, I took one look at the cluttered seat, messy with textbooks, pens stuck into the cracks, and complained, "Daddy, when are you going to get this cleaned already?"

This time, he didn't scoop up his things but made a nasty, sucking noise with his teeth and slammed the door shut. "Why you have to pick on me?" he yelled.

"And why can't you do things right?" I yelled back.

"I earn my wage! I send you to school! It's you who don't do things right! I didn't come to this country to hear this from my own daughter! What kinda daughter are you, criticizing your father all the time?"

We stared at one another. My father's chest rose up and down. His black eyes flickered once at me, then at his shoes. He made that sucking noise again. I hated him at that moment.

The next thing I knew he was stalking away from our house.

"Where are you going?" I called.

"You see," he said.

"Daddy, please!"

"You see what your old man got to say about this!"

"Forget it already!"

He had reached the Hellers' apartment and banged on their knocker. We stood there for what seemed like forever. Do something, I thought. But I could think of nothing short of turning on my heel and fleeing.

When the door swung open, the Hellers' maid stood on the threshold, wiping her hands in a towel. For the first time I saw that my father looked a bit like her, with her heavy, dark features, a scowl across her eyebrows. She didn't say a word as we were ushered inside, then disappeared on rubber-soled shoes.

Sol came into the room, looking like a genial TV Dad as he held out a hand. "Hello, Reginald. Why don't you sit down?"

He sat on a canvas chair, diagonally across from my father, who slouched on the couch. Elizabeth and I clambered onto a lounge chair strung with bristly cords. It felt as if we'd have to shout to hear one another.

"You want to tell me what happened?"

In short, anguished bursts, my father began his sorry tale of Parents Night, and his terrible disobedient daughter. Before he got very far, though, Sol held up a palm and said, "I'm very glad you've given me an opportunity to discuss this matter. Elizabeth's mother and I are also very concerned."

A relieved smile showed on my father's face.

"It appears this teacher is a real right-winger," Sol went on.

The smile faded. "But my daughter—"

"I can assure you, Reginald, I've already started some actions."

My father let out a few feeble remarks, chewing out phrases like "hard-work-and-what's-it-all-got-me-but-a-sassy-mouth-girl," but Sol didn't seem to hear. He kept dropping other kinds of words about "district rulings" and "petitions" and "parental pressure."

"Yeah, time I put a little pressure on this headstrong gal," my father agreed.

Sol kept going, while my father slumped in the flat cushions of the couch. He had not removed his coat and I noticed faded stains around his zipper. He crossed a leg, showing a tiny, ragged hole in his shoe. I began to have trouble following Sol's voice. I could not help feeling that Sol was not really talking to my father. His lips moved, but his body remained angled away from him. The sight was heartbreaking to me. I was used to hating my father, loving Sol.

Soon I stopped listening and stared at everyone's hands. I noticed my father's hand, especially. It was limp and curved, on its side. I thought about all my father had been forced to do with this hand, learn to use a fork and knife the American way, use paper napkins, scrub a toilet. It occurred to me how far a hand can travel; how it can tell the truth and lie as well. Then I noticed Sol's fingers making vague motions in front of his face and Elizabeth's hand tucked under her thighs.

Finally, my father rose from his chair. He stood in the middle of the room, patiently waiting for Sol to finish. Eventually, Sol trailed off, embarrassed. My father's brow was knit into a thoughtful scowl. He did not look angry, but tired, as if pulling from some deeper part of himself. He spoke in a clear and simple way, the voice he used when explaining an algebra problem to a particularly slow student. "Let me explain something, Sol," he said. "I come to this country seventeen years ago and this beautiful place take me into its arms. You know at my school they take me and treat me like a son? I proud to sing that song. And my daughter, she got to be proud too."

Sol wiped his hands on his trousers. "That's all very well and good but there's a more important issue at stake here—"

"She got to sing."

A silence opened between them, bright and round as a bottle. Into it flowed all the words I knew Sol thought about my father; how he was simple and wasn't the kind of man you could invite to a dinner party or ask onto a volunteer board. He wasn't someone you could introduce by saying, "Meet my friend Reginald. He's from the West Indies and he's also this terrific civil rights lawyer." Or, "He's a famous actor and he can sing calypso." My father was simply himself, a math teacher with a hole in his shoe. Sol's eyes glittered. My own eyes hurt from seeing so hard into so many things.

Outside, the air was cold. My father's face no longer wore the ashamed expression he'd been carrying around for the past few weeks. He began to walk back to our apartment, without saying a word to me. It was early evening and the sun was setting, lighting up his arms, his legs. His black hair blew in the breeze. Then I saw it: a rim of sadness, of foreignness I wanted to dive inside. I began to run, hard, flinging my arms tight around his waist, hearing his startled laugh as I pulled that luminous difference deep inside myself.

The next Thursday morning, I did as I was told. I struggled into my scratchy, navy wool skirt and my white shirt with the cardboard collar that made my neck sweat. And thick white stockings with a chain of red roses latched up the sides. In the bathroom, I let my mother clip barrettes into my hair and fold a cotton hankie with THURSDAY embroidered in one comer. "Smooth your brow," she told me, "Why do you have to look so worried, like your father?"

At assembly, I sat next to Elizabeth. She was dressed in an orange-popsicle-colored shirt and her white hip-huggers, like any ordinary day. "It's too bad your Dad said all that," she whispered, nodding toward my skirt.

My hands cramped in my lap and I turned away. I had never sweated so hard.

The sixth-graders trooped in last, in dungarees washed to a snowy softness, sweaters with just the right amount of droop—the kind of outfits my mother wouldn't let me wear. "Ragamuffins," she called them.

They stood in a row with slight, knowing smiles on their lips and winked at Elizabeth, who smiled back. All week long, there had been phone calls, meetings, even a new mimeo-graphed leaflet that smelled of fresh ink. Sol Heller had already been to the principal. Sol Heller was planning to take PS 117 and the Hamster and anyone else who got in his way to court.

The singing began. It was raggedy and uneven, from too few voices. I stared at the sixth-graders' faces. They looked to me as if they were full of excellent thoughts, about bombs and massacres and Vietnam and babies. They were thinking of how good they were and even the bad singing that surrounded them seemed part of this same world where right and wrong, singing and not singing, were beautifully clear.

"You did a nice job," the Hamster told us at the end of the ceremonies. She glared at the rear rows. "Considering."

Then we all thronged into the yard for recess, like colored sand pouring on to concrete. First-graders, fourth-graders, and last of all, the sixth-grade girls who coolly slid off their arm-bands. The air exploded with shouts, blue ties twisted off, girls scratching at their uncomfortable dresses. I watched while the sixth-grade girls surged around Elizabeth. They touched her shoulders, her elbows, her head, as if she was already elusive. Her brown hair shone like silk in the sun.

After that, Elizabeth didn't come around much. The Hellers began to take her with them to their parties, so I stayed alone more often. My own house broke into silent, painful cells. My father slept too many hours a day; my mother began taking night courses at Queens College. I stopped badgering him and he soon slid into his old ways, forgetting to take out the garbage, the living room cluttered with his papers. And my mother stayed in the kitchen downstairs, elbows jabbing the air. We were an odd family, always fighting, not sure who we were meant to be.

My mischief turned inward, and I became shyer, more watch-ful. I did strange things, unacceptable things. I befriended boys who didn't live in Windsor Parks. Not the nice kind; boys who lit firecrackers in bottles or twisted off car ornaments.

With my mother's Polaroid camera, I began spying, taking pictures of the Hellers' parties or when Elizabeth played with other friends in the backyard. Sometimes I mailed the photos to Elizabeth's new friends and wrote on the back, STAY AWAY FROM MY WINDOW.

By junior high, I became the sort of person who collected details about other peoples' lives. In school I kept a notebook on every other kid and all my teachers. I wrote things like, "Mrs. Schuldenfrei wears false eyelashes and probably weighs about one hundred forty pounds. I know for a fact that she is dating two men and she is thirty-one and unmarried." About Johanna James, a girl from Barbados, I wrote, "She is too tall for her own good and shouldn't wear high heels. I have noticed three different boys, really men with raincoats and cars, pick her up after school. She is beautiful but not so smart. Even though she was voted seventh-grade Vice President, I don't think she'll ever go to college."

I would go through each kid in the class and jot down every bit of information I could think of. After I read back my notes, I felt myself float up above the identical garden apartment roofs, belonging nowhere, on my way somewhere. I spent a lot of hours walking up and down the Windsor Park streets, lonely, unhappy, aware of myself in ways I hadn't noticed before: my funny, pigeon-toed walk, just like my father's. My stare, trying to see into things that were ugly, never said. And there was also my habit of scrunching my face into a frown, as if permanently annoyed at a world that had cheated me of something I could not yet name.

ALONE AND ALL TOGETHER

Joseph Geha

ᐖ

Chicago, Illinois

I'm half way out the door, already late for school, but I can't just ignore a ringing phone. Mom picks up in the bedroom at the same time I do here in the kitchen. It's my sister, Sally, calling to say she's okay, not to worry.

I am confused. Mom's home from work for the second day in a row, all glum and remote from one of her relapses ... and *Sally's* okay?

"I know you are, Sweetie," Mom says from the bedroom phone. Her voice actually creaks from disuse.

"No, Mom," Sally says. "Don't you have the TV on?" She gives us that impatient, exasperated sigh of hers that I haven't missed one bit in the week she's been gone to visit Dad and his new wife in Brooklyn. I can just see her rolling her eyes. "Turn on the *TV.*"

Mom gets out of bed. First time in two days. "What channel?"

"Doesn't matter what channel," Sally says. "Any channel."

Both of us go to the TV room and then I see why. It is a sunny Tuesday morning, September the eleventh, and right there on live television the twin towers of the World Trade Center in New York are burning black smoke. The heat is so intense, a newscaster is saying, that people are jumping. Holding hands and jumping. I turn away in case the camera zooms in. Outside our kitchen window, above the tarred roofs of the red brick buildings across the street, there's a view of the very top of the Sears Tower. The double antennas shine white in the sunlight. Behind me, Mom gasps, and starts in with the Arabic, *Udrub!* and *Ya harram!*—Old Country expressions of amazement and horror that Sitti, my grandma, used to say. Any other time I'd be embarrassed, but now as I turn back to the TV, her cries don't sound excessive at all. *Don't let it be us,* the words just pop into my head like a prayer. *Let it be those white supremacists, again, like from Idaho or wherever. And not us.*

Now the local news on WGN is reporting that, due to threatening phone calls, Muslim and Arab parents are leaving work to bring their kids home from school. I think of my friend Jamila. We started hanging around together when I began taking Arabic lessons. Just last year she decided to start wearing the scarf they call *hijab,* and she's had some hassle about that already, kids making fun of her.

Mom asks me to put on the tea kettle, complaining her mouth feels dry. She's got those rings around her eyes again, and she moves like an old woman. The new medications do that. She's taking a combination now, what her doctor calls a cocktail. The one drug that's supposed to help lift her spirits hasn't kicked in yet, and the other one, which is supposed to calm her down, is working a little too well, if you ask me. I set her up on the sofa with pillows and a blanket. On TV they show it again and again, the one tower burning and the plane going into the other tower, and each time I want to turn away. The newscasters tell us about the Pentagon and then, a *fourth* plane in Pennsylvania. And then right on TV, right while I'm pouring the tea for Mom, we watch one of the towers slowly begin crashing down on itself, like in those timed demolitions. Mom throws off the blanket, wants to call Sally again. The phone lines to New York are all so jammed, she keeps getting busy signals before she even finishes dialing. Mom says I can stay home from school.

I want to call Jamila but Mom yells to stay off the phone because what if Sally is trying to reach us? It's not like we don't have call waiting. Still, I don't want to upset her more than she already is.

But then we both start crying when the newscasters tell us about the firemen who were in the building when it went down, how the signal devices attached to their gear are going off because they haven't moved. The rescuers say they can hear beepers too, and cell phones ringing beneath the rubble.

The Sears Tower is evacuated, then all the downtown. I'd like to see that. I turn to say so to Mom, but she is asleep. It's such a peaceful, beautiful day out, I want to get on a train and go down to the Loop and walk the empty streets. Cross over to Grant Park and have Buckingham Fountain all to myself. Maybe stroll down to the shore. Lake Michigan turns a deep green-blue when it's sunny like this. But then my heart sinks, imagining everything so quiet, so empty, and me alone in the middle of it all.

A few hours later, Sally calls back, again using Dad's cell phone. She tells us that the smoke has been coming their way all morning and they have to put wet towels under the apartment door and the window sills to keep it out. "We're all okay, though," she says, meaning herself and Dad. And his new wife.

Mom is on one extension, me stretching the cord on the other so I can keep an eye on the TV screen through the kitchen archway, and Sally far away in New York, all three of us watching the same thing, the strip at the bottom of the screen which is saying now that everything points to the hijackers being Middle Eastern extremists.

"I just wish they wouldn't say it's us," I say, "until they're, like, *sure*."

"Us?" my sister says. "What us?"

"You know what I mean."

"No, I don't. We were born here, and so were Mom and Dad, right here in Chicago, Illinois, U.S.A."

You're not here, I want to remind her. I am.

"What I want to know," Sally goes on, "is when 'us' stops meaning *ibn Arab* and starts meaning American!"

Maybe my sister is right—*ibn Amerkain!* Any other time I'd laugh, but now I just say, *"Tch,"* a tongue click, which is something I learned from her. *Tch* is her way of winning an argument. No matter what you say back you're wrong, is what *tch* means.

"What's going on there now?" Mom asks.

Sally has to deliver another one of her sighs before she can start telling us about how all she can see now is the smoke that's blowing their way from the World Trade Center. "Soon as we go outside," she says, "our eyes start stinging." Something about her voice is different. As if she's talking about somebody else's eyes stinging. "The streets are so quiet for Brooklyn."

"Here too," I say, and begin to explain how quiet it is now that the planes have stopped coming in at Midway Airport, which is just a couple miles from our apartment house, but Sally interrupts, saying great, that's all we need is for everybody to get into a big panic. The whole world's blowing up around us, and she sounds annoyed. I look at Mom, but her eyes are closed as she listens. It's scary when your own family acts like they don't want to see what you see. Like one of those nightmares when there's danger and your family is all smiling and normal, and you're the only one who sees it.

It feels like the time Dad sat us down to explain why they were divorcing. They'd married too young, he said, and so they grew out of love. I remember looking over at Sally, my *big* sister, and there she was nodding her head and playing along as if, sure, that made all the sense in the world. But me, I was like, *excuse* me? You *fall* in love? And then you *grow* out of it? Like, hel-*lo*-o?

The reason Sally's even in New York is that Dad flew her out so she could start looking at colleges in the City. She's a senior this year and has perfect grades. I'm a freshman, and I won't go into my opinion of perfect grades.

Sally told me before she left that Dad had already talked to her about maybe living out there. Stay with them for a while and see if she likes the city. To take a little of the stress off Mom, he said. Fine with me. But my sister believing that they'd actually want her to move in with them just goes to so show what a denier she is. They're practically newlyweds, Dad and his new wife. I'm so sure they want a teenage daughter sharing their tiny two-bedroom love nest.

"Everything's closed," Sally is going on in that same annoyed-sounding voice, "even that Italian place Dad keeps promising to take me to."

"Like, going out to eat is really important now?" I say. It's just an observation, but it sets her off.

"Nobody's talking to you," Sally says, taking her big sister tone with me. "And stop saying 'like,'" she adds. "It's *so* junior high."

Now Dad takes the phone. "Okay, you two," he says. As soon as he does, Mom turns quiet, so I end up having to talk to him. And I've got to admit, I find just the sound of his deep voice calms me down. Hearing it, I want to be home. But I *am* home. Does that make sense?

When Sitti, our grandmother, was alive, she used to look at Sally and me when we were quarreling and show us the Arabic gesture *sabr*, thumb and two fingers pressed together, meaning *patience*. Which is something our family never had a lot of. For a while after the divorce Mom used to get angry and start throwing things whenever the slightest thing frustrated her, a framed photograph that wouldn't stay up, a wine glass that happened to be in the wrong place at the wrong time.

Sitti came to live with us soon after Dad left. Things eventually settled down. Then last winter Dad announced he was getting remarried. Mom looked like she was about to begin throwing things again, starting with the phone in her hand, but she didn't. Instead she seemed to just sink back down into herself. Finally, she began seeing a therapist. She's on medication now, and it seems to be helping, but there are still days she can't get out of bed. Sometimes I look at her gazing at some empty space above the TV, and I think depression is just another way of going away.

Sally kind of went away when she was fifteen. That is, the old Sally. One day it was like somebody'd waved a magic wand over her. All of a sudden there's the new Sally, this *stranger*, who was either rolling her eyes at something you said that was "so lame," or else just sitting there all mean at the dinner table. You'd call her name and she'd snap back "Wha-at?" in this totally rude voice. Sitti said that she'd grow out of it in time and be like "the other beebles" again. Maybe, but she hasn't so far, and it's scary watching your older sister go through a change that you yourself are headed for. I told Sitti that if I ever got like Sally to just take me out and shoot me. She said she would. "Okay, I do dat, *habibti*," she said, which is Arabic for *sweetheart*.

Sitti didn't always exactly understand what you were saying. She came to America late and then she'd mostly lived not far from here in Chicago's 'Little Arabia' around Sixty-third and Kedzie where you can shop and do everything else in Arabic. When she did speak English, it was with a thick accent, *dis* and *dat*, *beebles* for people because Arabic doesn't have a "P" sound. And always with the Arabic expressions mixed in, *inshallah*, meaning God willing, and *hoost* for be quiet; and when she called us by name it was our Arabic names—Salma, not Sally, and Labibeh, not Libby. What she called us most of the time, though, were Arabic endearments—*ahlbi*, my heart, *adami*, my bones, *ya rohi*, my life breath. They can be so embarrassing when you translate them into English, but hearing them in Arabic always made me feel a part of her. She called us that, too, *ya ba'adi*, which means oh-part-of-me; and there was another one I thought was really strange, *ti'breeni*, which means bury me. Which we did. Sitti had a heart attack one afternoon while she was watching "All My Children," and she died in her favorite chair. That was last May. The week before prom.

Sitti had blue eyes, like me, which isn't unheard of among *ibn Arab* from Syria, but most Americans don't know that. Sitti said that when my mother was a little girl her hair looked just like mine, wavy and light, almost blonde. My sister has our father's black, curly, curly hair that she hates and I always wished for. Dad still jokes that Sally is his Arab daughter and I'm the American one. Which is funny because I'm the one who used to help Sitti cook *loubyeh* and *kusa* and *beitenjan mihshee*; I'm the one who goes with Jamila two nights a week to the mosque to learn to read and write Arabic—something neither he nor Mom can do. Our family isn't even religious, though Sally and I were baptized in the Melkite Rite. And that's something else that surprises people, Christian Arabs!

So I may look like the American one, but it's my sister Sally who always refused to answer Sitti in Arabic, and who kept saying "Not *this* again!" when she served us her special Sunday chicken stuffed with rice and lamb *heshweh*. There's hot dogs in the fridge, Mom would offer.

After the divorce, Dad changed his last name from Tammouz to Thomas. Rasheed Tammouz became Richard Thomas. For business reasons, he said. Sally and me, our last name is still Tammouz. Mom's, too. His new wife is blue-eyed like me and blonde, but a lot blonder. Her name is Dusty. Honest.

I see myself as a cheerful person, basically, a don't-just-sit-there-do-something person, which is probably why I don't have the nightmares that Jamila and Erin and some of my other friends tell me they've been having every night, airplanes chasing them, buildings tumbling down on them. I wake up each morning the way I always do, reaching around for the snooze button so I can drift just five minutes more. Not until I'm out of bed and heading for the bathroom does "it" come back to me. That's when my cheerfulness sort of fizzles away. A shiver runs through me, and I am back in this world again. What I have are *day*mares. Brushing my hair, I imagine myself at Ground Zero, digging with my bare hands.

The planes have begun flying again, roaring over our roof down toward Midway. I don't know if it's the medication kicking in finally or what, but Mom seems to improve over the weekend. Monday morning she drops me off on her way to work. I'd like a little music but she keeps the radio on Chicagoland, an all-news station. All week there have been reports of "incidents" mostly in the southwest suburbs where a lot of the *ibn Arab* live: in Bridgeview, just to the north of us, three hundred people waving American flags and chanting "USA! USA!" tried to march on the Mosque Foundation; three of the demonstrators were arrested. In Oak Lawn, not far from Bridgeview, kids gathered outside the high school waving flags and shouting anti-Arab insults at passing cars. A firebomb was tossed at the Arab American community center where Jamila and I take Arabic lessons. Luckily, just the doors were damaged and nobody was hurt. In Palos Heights, just to the east, a man attacked a Moroccan gas station attendant with a machete.

Mom shakes her head, but she still won't let me change the station. At a red light I watch people in the crosswalk on their way to work. Some of them glance over at us. I stare back at them through the windshield. They don't know us, what we are, and I'm glad. I'm ashamed that I'm glad. As the local news ends, the reporter reminds us that the Sears Tower is the tallest building in the United States. "Does that," the reporter asks, "make Chicago the next target?"

At school we talk about "the events" in almost every class. The teachers are all careful, of course, and so are the kids who speak up, but I wonder if polite is how they feel down deep. Especially the quiet ones. Now and then I overhear some things in the halls. You can tell when people are being mean and when they're just teasing. Like whenever Tyrone, who's black, calls me a camel jockey because of my name, Labibeh

Tammouz. There's no meanness in it. I know he likes me. And I just tease him back. But some names cross the line. Sand nigger. Raghead. Usually whenever I hear them I get real mad real fast and I don't care who knows it, but now just the thought of somebody saying them scares me a little, too. In Western Civ., Jamila is still wearing her *hijab* scarf, and when she sits next to me, I try to give her an encouraging smile. But I wish she would take that thing off. Okay. She was born in Egypt, and she's a Muslim, but she's an American, too. She's in honors classes with me and her English is just about perfect.

When I get home, Mom is on the phone again with Sally and I pick up the extension. People are helping each other in New York, Sally says, raising money, restaurants sending hot food down to the workers at Ground Zero. Lots of people were displaced because of all the debris, and New Yorkers are opening their homes, putting them up. Something about Sally's voice makes me stop paying attention so much to what she's saying—how cards and flowers are being left at firehouses all over Manhattan, and how everywhere you see flags flying—and I listen to the tone of it, shaky almost, like on the edge of something, tears, maybe, or anger. "Every day there's another memorial service, another vigil," she says, sounding about to go trembly.

"How about you, Sweetie?" Mom asks. "Are you going to any of the services?"

"Me?" Sally asks in a sharp little cry, angry or sad, I can't tell which. Neither can Mom, who glances up at me through the kitchen archway. "I can't believe you're saying that. What do you guys expect me to do, go to church or something?" The way Sally says "you guys," I realize that Dad must be right there in the room with her, and she's saying this to both our parents, blaming them for her lack of comfort. Blaming them for not raising us religious, maybe. And maybe it's also for the dark eyes they gave her, the olive skin and the dark, curly hair. Down deep, though, it's for having to feel alone in all this. That part I'm sure of because I feel it, too.

"It helps if you feel you're part of a community," Mom says in her soothing therapy voice.

Big mistake. "As if you'd know what that's like!" Sally says, her voice breaking into tears. "You're not even *around* anymore!" I hear Dad in the background, trying to comfort her. She's sobbing so hard she doesn't even say "I love you" before we hang up.

Hyde Park is just a few streets over, down near the University. There are bookstores there and coffee shops and delis and places that sell used vintage clothing. It's where my friends and I usually go to hang out, but today the streets feel different. For one thing, there's nowhere near the usual crowds. My friend Erin says it because everybody's still glued to CNN. Not me. I'm *glad* to get out of the house, away from the TV.

Except for school, this is the first time I've been out all week. School is school, but here is different. It's like being in the world. I had asked Jamila to come with us—-our usual Arabic lessons have been suspended because of threats to the mosque-- but her mother was afraid of trouble. On the phone we complained about how unfair that was, but now I'm sort of relieved. Even though I don't look like her, I still keep getting this creepy sense that people passing by are turning and noticing me, as if they can detect Arabic in my brain, or something. I tell my friend Erin that, laughing, hoping she'll laugh too, and she does. We've been friends since second grade.

"If anybody's looking," Erin says, "they're looking at the *dib* over there, not you."

Erin is American, and *dib* is a word she picked up from me. It's Arabic for *bear*, but really meaning a huge, clumsy guy, like an oaf. Coming out of a dollar store is Jamila's little brother, Ahmed. Only he's not so little. Still in junior high, he's over six feet tall and walks all hunched over as if he's not aware how goofy he looks with one shirttail hanging out. Exactly a *dib*. I notice his shoelaces are untied. The way he's hurrying out of the store, he's practically falling over himself. "Hey," I say to Erin. "I know him."

"You do?"

Before I can answer, I realize that Ahmed is trying to get away from three guys who followed him out of the store. He looks scared. "Just tell us where you're from!" a little guy is saying. He has a tight rubber-band voice. Ahmed stops and turns. The two others stay behind the little guy, who seems to enjoy showing them how easy this is.

"Chicago," Ahmed answers, so quietly I can hardly hear him. He has no accent at all. As he makes as if to move on, the little guy steps closer, backing him up against a display window.

"So are you or aren't you?"

Erin grabs my arm, and I look around for help. But people are just walking by like everything's normal. *Do something,* I think, and I start to take mental snapshots, trying to see and remember. They're ordinary guys, I imagine myself telling the officers. They all have on ball caps turned backwards. The guy doing the talking is wearing one of those shiny tight muscle shirts.

"Am I what?"

"You know what I mean." Ahmed turns but the little guy keeps facing him. "I said, you know what I mean!" His teeth clench as he speaks, his lips barely move.

I know what he means, too. Ahmed's olive skin. His brown eyes and dark curly hair. Darker even than my sister's.

"Why do you care?" Ahmed says. He begins to walk away. The guy almost steps back but then he gives a shove that spins Ahmed up against a display window, his shirttail flapping.

"Hey, I'm still talking to you." Now people are stopping to look. He begins waving his hand right in front of Ahmed's face, like imitation slaps, and Ahmed puts an arm up to protect himself. Instantly, the little guy's hand snaps out and grasps Ahmed by the wrist.

"Just say it—you are or you aren't." I watch his knuckles turn white with squeezing.

Ahmed tries to yank his arm away but the guy holds on and raises his other hand in a fist. I hear one of his friends say, "Raghead."

I look at Erin next to me, but she's making little swallowing noises like she can't talk. And then there I am stepping in. I don't even know what I'm doing, I'm just doing it, angling myself face-to-face with the little guy. "You let him go!" I say. My voice surprises me. It doesn't come out screechy, like I feel, but low and strong. People begin stopping now, a small crowd forming. Ahmed just blinks. I'm not sure he even realizes who I am.

The little guy is stunned for a second, but just for a second. Then he and his friends start to laugh. I don't care, so long as they leave Ahmed alone. "You losers!" I yell at them. That makes them laugh harder, but I step even closer and the little guy actually steps back, looking at me the way you look at a crazy person and wonder what they're going to do next. I'm wondering that myself when I hear somebody call out "Whew!" We all turn and look. Some middle-aged woman in the crowd, a University type with a bandanna in her hair. She's giving me a you-go-girl smile. Everybody else, shoppers, deli clerks, a panhandler, they're all watching. I look up at a man in a white apron standing behind me, silent, poker-faced. Nothing's going to happen to me or to Ahmed. I can see that in the set of his jaw.

The little guy must see it, too. He opens his fingers and lets go of Ahmed's wrist. He and his friends don't say a word, they just back off and walk away cocky, looking people in the eye so they'll make way. That's how you walk when you know you should be ashamed of yourself but won't admit it.

When they're gone, Ahmed is still standing there, jaw hanging open. Breathing through his mouth. I go up to him and touch his wrist. The poor *dib*.

Going home, I see the Sears Tower everywhere I look. Out the bus window. Over my shoulder as I round the corner onto my street. Like it's following me home. Finally I stop and turn, right there on my front stoop, and I look up at it. Lit against the dark sky, its high beacons point right to Chicago, to us. Yes, it could happen here next time. And yet people are up there again, working. People are in airplanes, too, flying again. Being afraid is catching, but so is being brave.

The minute I get home I want to call Jamila. As soon as the mosque school opens the two of us are going together for Arabic lessons again, I want her to know that. But Mom is on the phone with Sally.

"Then what happened?" Mom asks. There's a husky softness in her voice, like you get sometimes after a good cry. Did I miss something? I reach for the bedroom extension. Sally is talking about how the city had a minute of silence to honor the victims. People all up and down Park Slope stopped everything and just stood there. Cars pulled over to the curb. "For a whole minute all you could hear was the wind," she says. "Do you know how *long* a minute is?" And then the sirens started up. From all over the five boroughs. From all the firehouses and police precincts. All the squad cars and ambulances. It sounded to her like voices wailing, calling to one another across the city.

And that, Sally says, was when she saw the sign in a coffee shop window: the Arab American community over on Atlantic Avenue was having a candlelight vigil to honor the victims of September eleventh. "It was just one train stop away," she said.

"Oh, Sweetie," Mom says, real tender, then in Arabic, "*Ti'breeni.*"

"I was nervous to go there by myself," Sally says. "But as soon as I got off the train I found myself walking in a crowd. There were all nationalities. Muslim women. There were Asians. Lots of people with their children. And dogs. People stood outside their shops. Everyone was really respectful. We walked to the Promenade. People were praying. They held candles and pictures. Then everyone went quiet. The light was gleaming off the buildings across the river and off the column of smoke rising from where the World Trade Center once was. Every one of us. Mom, I was alone, and we were all together. Oh, it was such a beautiful day."

The phone is quiet a moment. I have a chance to ask now whether she's staying or not, but I figure I'll find out in good time. *Sabr*, Sitti used to say, *patience*. And she used to say *ti'breeni* to me too. Which means more than "bury me." I studied Arabic and I know that what it really means is more like *Live after me. Survive me.* What the ones we lost would want us to do. That's something. But I don't go into it now. Sally is crying and Mom's crying, and I just listen.

ABOUT THE AUTHORS

DUANE BIG EAGLE is an Osage poet and fiction writer, born in Claremore, Oklahoma. He has taught creative writing as part of the California Poets in the Schools program, and is the author of *Bidato: ten mile river poems, Theme for Ernie,* and *Birthplace: Poems & Painting.* He is a traditional Southern Straight dancer and a member of the Northern California Osage Association.

MARINA BUDHOS's most recent novels include *Watched,* which takes on surveillance in a post-9/11 era, and *The Long Ride,* which follows three mixed-race girls during a 1970s integration struggle. Among her many award-winning books include the young adult novels *Tell Us We're Home* and *Ask Me No Questions.* Budhos has been a Fulbright Scholar to India, received a Rona Jaffe Award for Women Writers, and two fellowships from the New Jersey Council on the Arts, among other honors. A graduate of Cornell and Brown, she is a professor of English at William Paterson University.

NORMA ELIA CANTÚ is a professor of English at the University of Texas in San Antonio. Alongside her writing of poetry and fiction, her publications on border literature, the teaching of English, quinceañera celebration, and the religious dance tradition matachines have earned her an international reputation as a scholar and folklorist. She has co-edited four books and edited a collection of testimonios by Chicana scientists, mathematicians, and engineers. Her award-winning *Canícula: Snapshots of a Girlhood en la Frontera* chronicles her childhood experiences on the border.

LAN SAMANTHA CHANG is the author of a collection of short fiction, *Hunger,* and two novels, *Inheritance* and *All Is*

Forgotten, Nothing Is Lost. She has received creative writing fellowships from Stanford, Princeton, the Radcliffe Institute for Advanced Study, the Guggenheim Foundation, and the National Endowment for the Arts. She is the Program Director of the Iowa Writers' Workshop.

SANDRA CISNEROS is an activist poet, short story writer, novelist, essayist, and artist who explores the lives of the working-class. She has won National Endowment for the Arts fellowships in both poetry and prose, a MacArthur Fellowship, and the 2015 National Medal of Arts presented by President Barak Obama. Her books include, *The House on Mango Street, Woman Hollering Creek and Other Stories,* and *Caramelo.* A dual citizen of Mexico and the United States, she currently lives in Guanajuato.

TOPE FOLARIN graduated from Morehouse College and the University of Oxford in England, where he was a Rhodes Scholar. Born in Ogden, Utah, the son of Nigerian immigrants, he was the first writer based outside Africa to win the Caine Prize for African Writing, for his short story "Miracle." He currently works at the Institute for Policy Studies, focusing on African politics and the racial/wealth divide in the United States. His forthcoming first novel is entitled *A Particular Kind of Black Man.*

RIVKA GALCHEN was born in Canada and grew up in Oklahoma. She is the award-winning author of three books, *American Innovations* (stories), *Atmospheric Disturbances* (novel), and *Little Labors* (essays). Her fiction and essays frequently appear in *The New Yorker, Harper's, The London Review of Books,* and *The New York Times.* She received an M.D. at Mt. Sinai School of Medicine and an M.F.A. at Columbia University, where she now teaches writing.

JOSEPH GEHA was born in Lebanon and raised in the United States. He is the author of *Through and Through: Toledo Stories,* a collection of short stories inspired by his experiences of growing up in an émigré Arab American community, and *Lebanese Blonde,* a novel. His fiction has been chosen for inclusion in the Permanent Collection, Arab-American Archive, of the Smithsonian Institution. He is professor-emeritus at Iowa State University.

VEERA HIRANANDANI grew up in the 1980s, in a small town in Connecticut. Her mother is Jewish American and her father is from a Hindu family in India. She graduated from George Washington University, then earned her M.F.A. in fiction writing at Sarah Lawrence College. Hiranandani is the author of the award-winning novels *The Night Diary* and *The Whole Story of Half a Girl,* as well as the series *Phoebe G. Green.* She teaches creative writing at Sarah Lawrence College's Writing Institute.

LANGSTON HUGHES was born in Joplin, Missouri. His first published work appeared the year after his high school graduation. Hughes played a central role in the Harlem Renaissance and the Civil Rights movement, and won countless awards for his poetry, novels, plays, columns, and social activism. He was an innovator of an art form called jazz poetry. Among Hughes's books are *The Big Sea, Simple Speaks His Mind, The Ways of White Folk,* and *The Weary Blues.*

GISH JEN's given name was Lillian, but in high school her friends nicknamed her "Gish" after the actress Lillian Gish. She has received numerous awards and honors, including a Guggenheim Fellowship and the Mildred and Harold Strauss Award from the American Academy of Arts and Letters. Her short stories have been published in *The New Yorker, The Atlantic,* and in dozens of other periodicals and anthologies. Her novels were featured in a PBS American Masters special on the American novel. Among them are *Typical American,* a finalist for the National Book Critics Circle Award, and *Mona in the promised land.*

FRANCISCO JIMÉNEZ was born in Tlaquepaque, Mexico. When he was four years old, his family emigrated to Santa

Maria, California. From a young age, he worked as a migrant field hand, attending school only when harvest season was over in November. When he was fifteen, he was deported to Mexico, but he returned to graduate from high school with honors and to become a United States citizen. He is currently a professor at Santa Clara University and the author of several books, including *The Circuit, Breaking Through,* and the memoir *Taking Hold: From Migrant Childhood to Columbia University.*

EDWARD P. JONES was born in Washington, D. C. in 1950. He earned a B.A. from Holy Cross, an M.F.A. from the University of Virginia, and worked in publishing for several decades. During this time, he wrote the stories that would become his first book, *Lost in the City,* which won the PEN/Hemingway Award in 1992. For his first novel, *The Known World,* he was awarded a Pulitzer Prize and a MacArthur Fellowship in 2004. His most recent book is the short story collection, *All Aunt Hagar's Children.* Jones teaches writing at George Washington University.

TOSHIO MORI was born in Oakland, California, in 1910 and was the first Japanese-American to publish a book of short stories in the United States. Scheduled to debut in 1942, his collection *Yokohama, California* was delayed until 1949 by the Second World War. During the war, Mori was held in the Topaz Relocation Center in Utah, an internment camp for Americans of Japanese descent and immigrants from Japan. While there, he wrote for the camp newspaper and was the camp historian. Mori worked in a small family nursery for most of the rest of his life, and wrote two more books, *The Chauvinist and Other Stories* and *The Woman from Hiroshima.*

MARY K. MAZOTTI was born in California in 1924. Her parents were immigrants from a Calabrian village, and she spent her childhood among other immigrant Italians who came from the same area. She is the mother of seven children. For many years, she worked as a school secretary. In 1981, she began to write, and has been published in various journals.

NAOMI SHIHAB NYE grew up in St. Louis, Missouri; Jerusalem; and San Antonio, Texas, where she now lives. She is an honored poet, the recipient of Lannan, Guggenheim, and Witter Bynner fellowships, among other awards, and the author of many books of poetry for adults, as well as poetry and novels for children and young adults. Among her published works are *Habibi: A Novel* and *Sitti's Secrets*, a picture book that is based on her experiences of visiting her beloved grandmother in Palestine. Her book *19 Varieties of Gazelle: Poems of the Middle East* was a finalist for the 2002 National Book Award. She has also edited several distinguished anthologies. Nye has taught writing and worked in schools all over the world, including in Muscat, Oman.

SUSAN POWER was born in 1961 in Chicago, Illinois, and is a member of the Standing Rock Tribe of the Dakotas. Power attended Harvard University for her B.A. and her J.D. After a short career in law, she decided to become a writer. She earned her M.F.A. from the Iowa Writers' Workshop, and her debut novel, *The Grass Dancer*, won the 1995 Hemingway Foundation/PEN Award for Best First Fiction. Power has published several other books and short stories, and currently teaches at Hamline University in St. Paul, Minnesota.

As a youth, GARY SOTO worked in the fields of the San Joaquin Valley. Although he was not a good student in high school, he developed an interest in writing and went on to publish more than forty books for children, young adults, and adults, including *Baseball in April, Living Up the Street, A Summer Life, Buried Onions,* and *A Fire in My Hands*. He is also an award-winning poet, and has been the recipient of fellowships from the Guggenheim Foundation and the National Endowment for the Arts (twice). His *New and Selected Poems* was a 1995 finalist for both the National Book Award and the Los Angeles Times Book Award. He lives in Berkeley, California.

JUSTIN TORRES was born in New York City in 1980. He has published short fiction in *The New Yorker, Harper's, Granta, Tin*

House, and *The Washington Post,* as well as nonfiction in *The Guardian* and *The Advocate.* His first novel, *We the Animals,* was made into a feature film. A graduate of the Iowa Writers' Workshop, he was a Wallace Stegner Fellow at Stanford University, a fellow at the Radcliffe Institute for Advanced Study at Harvard, and a Cullman Center Fellow at The New York Public Library. He is an Assistant Professor of English at University of California, Los Angeles.

MICHELE WALLACE was born in Harlem, the daughter of artist/author Faith Ringgold and the pianist/master printer Earl Wallace. She is Professor Emeritus at the City College of New York and the City University of New York Graduate Center, and the Founder and Director of The Faith Ringgold Society. Wallace earned a doctorate in Cinema Studies at New York University, and is the author of *Black Macho and the Myth of the Superwoman, Black Popular Culture: A Project by Michele Wallace, Dark Designs and Visual Culture,* and *Invisibility Blues: New Edition.* She is currently at work on a book to be called *The Mona Lisa Interview: Faith Ringgold's French and American Collections, 1990–1999.*

ABOUT THE EDITORS

ANNE MAZER is the author of forty-four books for young readers and writers. Among them are picture books such as *The Salamander Room* and *The No-Nothings and Their Baby*; novels, including *Moose Street* and *The Oxboy*; *A Sliver of Glass*, short stories; and two bestselling series for young readers, *The Amazing Days of Abby Hayes* and *Sister Magic*. Her *Spilling Ink: A Handbook for Young Writers*, co-authored with Ellen Potter, was an NCTE 2011 Notable Book in Language Arts. Mazer is also the editor of four anthologies about youth that are widely used in elementary through college classrooms: the original version of *America Street*; *Going Where I'm Coming From*, memoirs; *Working Days*, stories about teens at work; and *A Walk in My World*, international short stories.

BRICE PARTICELLI earned his Ph.D. from Columbia University where he was Director of the literacy-focused educational nonprofit, Student Press Initiative, working with underserved schools in New York City. He is a 2017 NYSCA/NYFA Artist Fellow in Nonfiction with the New York Foundation for the Arts, and has had work recently published in *The Common*, *The Big Roundtable*, *Travelers' Tales*, and *Fourth River*. He teaches writing at Pace University in New York City and is working on his first novel.

ACKNOWLEDGMENTS

The editors and the publisher wish to gratefully acknowledge the authors, literary agents, and publishers who granted us permission to reprint or publish for the first time the stories in this collection.

"The Journey," by Duane Big Eagle, copyright © 1983 by Duane Big Eagle. Reprinted by permission of the author.

"American Dad, 1969," by Marina Budhos, copyright © 2000 by Marina Budhos. First published in *Jahaji*, ed. Frank Birbal-Singh, TSAR Press. Reprinted by permission of the author. All rights reserved.

"Halloween," from *Canicula: Snapshots of a Girlhood on the Frontera, Updated Edition*, by Norma Elia Cantú. Copyright © 2015 by The University of New Mexico Press. Reprinted with the permission of the publisher.

"Water Names" from *Hunger: A Novella and Stories* by Lan Samantha Chang. Copyright © 1998 by Lan Samantha Chang. Used by permission of W. W. Norton & Company, Inc.

"Mericans," from *Woman Hollering Creek and Other Stories* by Sandra Cisneros. Copyright © 1991 by Sandra Cisneros. Published by Vintage Books, a division of Penguin Random House, New York, and originally in hardcover by Random House. Reprinted by permission of Susan Bergholz Literary Services, New York and Lamy, NM. All rights reserved.

"The Summer of Ice Cream," by Tope Folarin, copyright © 2014, 2019 by Tope Folarin. Originally published, in a different